ECHOES

A NOVEL BY MEGAN GANT

Copyright © 2022 Megan Gant

No part of this book may be reproduced or transmitted in any form or by any means, electronic or mechanical, including photocopying, recording or by any information storage or retrieval system, without written permission from the author and the publisher, except for the inclusion of a brief quotation in a review.

ISBN: 978-1-3999-1503-8

1

Detective Hart's eyes were burning into mine. She was staring me out. With each passing silent second, I could feel the blood beneath my skin getting hotter and hotter, my heart beating faster and faster until eventually I broke. The words seemed to fall out of my mouth, stumbling across the table to aimlessly then be absorbed by the Dictaphone sitting parallel between us.

Hart's face didn't soften as I gave the final details. Each sentence felt like a hard- hitting blow as if someone was physically punching me in the throat but to the woman opposite me it was like nothing was said at all. She begins to open her mouth and starts to talk but as soon as she does, an older woman with white hair and a suit, somewhat out of breath, comes blazing into the room. She tells the room she's my lawyer and forces them to stop recording, ushering them out of the room immediately. She trundles round the table and pulls the chair next to me and sits placing her briefcase on the table. She holds her hands out for me to shake, introducing herself but I can't hear anything. I ask her to repeat herself, so she does, but again nothing. Nothing but a faint high pitched ringing sound, getting higher and louder and higher and louder. All the sound from before seems to vanish into thin air.

My lawyer places her hands on both of my shoulders. She looks at me with so much concern in her eyes, mouthing words at me, but I can't seem to make any sense of them. The all-familiar tightness around my chest begins to return and I place my hand over my mouth, closing my eyes to try to at least gain some kind of composure, but this time nothing seems to work. I open my eyes once more and the lady in front of me is now shaking me violently, still mouthing something completely incoherent. I manage to find the air in my lungs for one deep inhale and my whole body jolts forward.

I look to my left and see Sebastian out for the count sprawled across his side of the bed. I run my hands through my hair and slowly make my way out of bed, grabbing my robe as I slip out of the bedroom door across the hallway and into the kitchen. The only light filling the apartment is the streetlight flickering from outside. Opening the fridge, I'm blinded. I grab the milk and pour it into the saucepan on the hob, while simultaneously adding cocoa powder to my favourite mug. Folding my arms around myself, I wait for the milk to warm.

'Can't sleep?' A hushed deep voice startles me. I look over my shoulder and see Charlie sitting on the sofa, encased in darkness. He gets up and shuffles himself over to the kitchen island, perching on a stool.

'Had another nightmare.' Charlie's brow furrows immediately, my attention turns back to the hob.

'Again? That's the third time this week Kate.' The milk in the pan begins to bubble slightly, I swirl it around before pouring it into the mug, creating the warm cocoa needed to hopefully send me back to sleep. I don't acknowledge Charlie's remark. Instead, just offer to make him a cocoa. He declines.

'You need to speak to someone about this. Someone that isn't me. Or Sebastian.' I gesture to sit back down on the sofa, a little further away from the bedroom in the hopes we don't wake sleeping beauty. I clutch my mug and stare back at Charlie.

'I know and I will. I want to wait until after the trial at least. It's just a bad dream.' 'It's not just a bad dream though is it. You've been having these flashbacks for weeks.

Have you told him?' Charlie gestures to Sebastian, who's still none the wiser in the other room.

'No. He thinks they've stopped.' I shuffle in my seat to face Charlie. He moves closer and pulls me into a hug.

'And why's that Kate?' I stay cuddled to his chest.

'Because I told him they had.' My words are a little muffled against his cotton shirt.

Charlie exhales trying to stifle a laugh. He pulls away and looks at me with a look of disapproval that only a brother could have.

'Don't lie to him. I know you're only trying to protect him. I've seen the way you've been acting around him recently, like everything is fine and that you're coping, but I know you're not. It's okay to not be coping Kate. You don't have to deal with this on your own. Not anymore. Promise me you'll tell him?' A lump in my throat forms, I try to gulp it away but to no avail.

'I promise.'

'And you promise to speak to someone?'

'I promise.' He pulls me back in for another hug before pulling away and yawning into his hands.

'How long have you been up for?' He yawns again.

'Only half hour before you.' The roles reverse briefly and I'm the one looking at him with a furrowed brow.

'You okay?' He leans forward, with his head bowed down.

'Couldn't sleep either. Nervous about tomorrow.' He reaches to the coffee table and checks his phone seeing that it's 2am. 'Well, today.'

I frown at him until it dawns on me. Visitation day. I dramatically lean back into the sofa sighing as my head hits the cushion behind me.

'I completely forgot. Do we have to go?' My brother leans back into the sofa joining me.

'We've missed the last two. We can't keep putting it off.' His quiet monotone reply fit the mood perfectly, but he was right. As much as we didn't want to see them, they had requested to see us. God knows why.

2

I roll over and almost fall off the side of the sofa. Looking up at the clock parallel to me on the wall, I see the metal hands informing me it's 05:45am. I slip off the knitted blanket laying over me and stretch myself from the sofa before walking back to my bedroom. I gently open the door, peeping my head around to see Sebastian still in a deep sleep, just as I left him 3 hours before. I tip toe into the room picking up a small hand towel before closing the door behind me softly. Walking down the corridor and into the bathroom, I turn the light on, and it blinds me momentarily. I stare at myself in the mirror. Running my hands through my hair, I pull the bed head knots apart with my fingers. I run the cold tap, cupping my hands underneath before leaning down and splashing my face with the water.

Looking back into the mirror, I hope that maybe doing so has changed the reflection back to how I remember it, but no luck. I dry my face before switching the light off, leaving the bathroom silently. I tip toe back into the bedroom I share with my boyfriend and sit at the dressing table. Trying my hardest to not look at the reflection in the oval mirror staring back at me, instead I look through the little wooden boxes sitting either side.

The first two boxes had little stud earrings in that I haven't worn in years. The third box had a small plastic bag folded in it. I pull it out and open the seal. Sitting there at the bottom was a gold ring with a ruby gemstone surrounded by tiny diamonds. I felt a lump form in my throat. Taking the ring out, I slip it on. Staring at it on my hand allows my brain to just stop for a bit. For a few seconds, none of the bad things that happened entered my train of thought. For a few seconds I felt comfort, I felt safe, I felt, dare I say it, like myself. We haven't spoken to or heard from Doreen ever since last summer but there is not one day I don't think about her. Movement behind me pulled me away from my thoughts, I look over my shoulder and see Sebastian turning over. I grab one of his oversized hoodies and slip it on, pulling the hood over my head before putting on a pair of my trainers and slipping out of the room once more.

Walking past the kitchen, I take Charlie's keys off the counter and put them in my pocket. Sebastian's coat hangs on the back of the armchair, and I rifle through looking for his wallet. The brown leather wallet is worn, but it flips open and there is a photo of us on the inside. I smile at it before taking the card linked to our joint account out and put the wallet back. I make my way out of the apartment as quietly as I can and head into the lift.

The winter sun is only just making an appearance as I walk down the back streets of Brooklyn, turning down a little street past nail salons and coffee shops, that in doubt will be open in a few hours. At the end of the road are mini marquees where independent businesses are setting up ready for market day. I walk along the pathway and reach the 24-hour pharmacy, the automatic doors welcome me in. I pick up a basket and aimlessly browse each aisle. There is something freeing about just wandering at leisure, it's most definitely the little things. I used to hate it when people said that. I get it now. It's the freedom. It's the magpie sitting in the tree. It's the pollen floating in the breeze. It's the kisses on your forehead. It's breathing a little deeper into your lungs and feeling it deep within your body.

I crouch down looking at the boxes of hair dye in front of me, I pick up 3 boxes of Dark Reddish-Brown dye and drop them into my basket, I stand back up and begin to walk around the shop again occasionally picking up the odd packet of candy as I go along.

Eventually I make my way to the checkout and leave the store, plastic bag in hand I walk across the road and into the Starbucks that had just opened it's doors.

'Three Venti Lattes please.' My voice is deep and a little groggy.

'Can I take a name?' the barista asks from over the counter, I must have been his first customer of the day.

'Rose.' I mumble back at her.

After 10 minutes of me awkwardly standing there staring at the floor and every now and then jumping as the café door opened, the drinks were ready. Kindly, the barista fashioned them into a cardboard carrier. Picking them up I scurried back out to the street. I aimlessly make my way back to the apartment making an effort to look up to the newly awoken sky to take in the buzzing of the city. The air gets colder by the second and before I know it, I'm being elevated back to my front door. I turn the key in the lock and almost instantly I'm greeted by two men turning around looking distressed. They both rush over to me and I'm startled by their physical affection towards me.

'Where have you been?' Sebastian pulls me into a tight hug, I try to not drop the fragile cups of coffee balancing in my hands.

'We've been calling you for an hour, you didn't pick up.' I pull away from the tight grip of Sebastian to see Charlie standing there, looking angry. Angrier than I've ever seen him.

'I went out for a walk and I got you both coffee. I didn't have my phone on me.' I walk past both men glaring at me and put the cups of coffee down on the kitchen island. I walked straight into the bedroom and put the bag of hair dye down on the bed and walked back out again and saw that the boys hadn't moved an inch and were just staring at each other. I walk back over, take my coffee from the counter and sit down on the sofa. They both just watch me with complete confusion on their faces.

They eventually join me with their coffees, Sebastian sitting next to me on the sofa and Charlie in the armchair opposite, his eyes scoping me out.

'How long were you gone for?' I look up at the clock hanging on the wall.

'Just over an hour. Didn't think I'd been that long. Sorry.' My words were blunt and my tone, mono.

'Where did you go?' I tilt my head to the side.

'The shop and then Starbucks, like I said when I came in. What's with the third degree?' Charlie takes a deep breath, Sebastian notices and places his hand on my leg. I flinch slightly but let him keep it there.

'We don't mean to interrogate you; we were just worried about you that's all. You've barely spoken to us recently and then this morning I woke up and you had disappeared, I thought something had happened, we both did.' I glance at both of them trying to think of what to say and before I can add anything to the conversation, Charlie speaks, his voice is deep and almost hushed.

'You're wearing the ring.' He gestures with his eyes to the Ruby ring sitting on my left hand.

'Yeah, I found it this morning in the dressing table. I wanted to wear it.' Charlie says nothing to reply but just simply smiles. I look back at Sebastian and I can see in his face he wants to ask questions, but he doesn't. He just sips his coffee.

I stand, rummaging in my pockets and hold out the bank card towards Sebastian. 'Here, I took it out of your wallet to buy the coffees.' He looks up at me with sympathetic eyes, I have to force him to take the card back. He mumbles a "thank you". 'I'm going to use the bathroom, does anyone want to use it before I go in?' They both simultaneously say no. I walk into my bedroom, pulling the plastic bag off the bed and scurrying into the bathroom closing the door behind me.

Running my hands through my hair, the plastic

gloves catching through any knots lingering in my hair, I saturate each section with the mixed dye, taking my time, yawning occasionally as the sun fully comes up. After about 45 minutes I run a bath, the steam fills the room as I step in. I lay down and rinse my newly tinted mahogany hair. The water quickly turns a muddy red as I sink further into the bath, the water covering my face.

My thoughts seem to fade away as hold my breath under the water for a little longer than I could hold out for. A banging started subtly echoing through the water until I felt hands clutching around my waist. My head jolted up out of the water and I gasped for air. Sebastian held me in the air for a brief second before I started screaming, pulling away from him and grabbing a towel, frantically wrapping it around me and folding my arms as Sebastian stares at me with tears in his eyes looking increasingly shocked at my reaction. Charlie scurries into the door frame standing behind Sebastian.

'What's going on?' Charlie's voice echoes slightly in the bathroom. Sebastian hesitates and tries to say something, but I speak first.

'He just grabbed me out of the bath! I was in here, washing my hair and he just came in and pulled me out of the bath!' My arms were stretched out pointing at Sebastian as I accuse him. Charlie pushes further into the small bathroom, placing his hand on Sebastian's shoulder, he turns round and looks at him.

'She'd been in here for ages, I knocked on the door and there wasn't an answer so I came in and her whole body was under the water and the water was that colour and I just thought the worst! I promise, I wouldn't have done this if I wasn't worried. You know that don't you?' He turns back round to me, reaching his hands out to me but I just back away further, the backs of my legs against the bath. Charlie notices I'm shaking and walks in front of me, he places his hands on my shoulders and I instantly relax.

'Go into your room, take your clothes, go get warm and dry your hair. I'll tidy up here.' I nod my head and duck out of the bathroom, trying to avoid any eye contact with Sebastian. Closing the bedroom door behind me, I press my ear up against it to see if I can hear anything. There's nothing but mumbling until I hear them step out into the main hall of the apartment.

'It's just, I'm worried about her Charlie. She's not been herself and when I opened the door I just panicked. You know I wouldn't do anything to hurt her. Ever.' Sebastian's voice is aching and a lump in my throat forms slightly as the thought of me causing him that pain hits me hard. I open the door slightly and peek through the crack, making sure they don't see me. The boys are facing each other, both with furrowed brows. Sebastian looking heartbroken.

'Bud. I know. I would have done the same if I had gone in, trust me, I would. Don't beat yourself up about it, it's going to take some time for Kate to get back to her old self.

You're doing everything you can.' Sebastian nods at Charlie's words, the lump in my throat is slowly getting significantly bigger.

'I knew it would be tough, but I just didn't expect her to shut off like this. The last few weeks she has been so jumpy, won't let me go near her. I put my hand on her leg earlier and she flinched. It breaks my heart. She was doing so well. I thought she was making progress since her nightmares ended.' I glance over at Charlie and his face instantly gave it away.

Sebastian sighed, scratching his head. 'How long have they been back for?' I slowly close the door, leaning my back against it before sliding down it, cradling my knees in my arms at just the thought of the truth coming out and Sebastian realising I'd been lying to him this whole time.

'Honestly? I don't think they've ever stopped. She had one this morning.' 'She didn't wake me up to tell me.'

'I don't think she's telling anyone. She only told me this morning because I was already awake myself and I questioned her.' Sebastian's gaze hits the floor. He clears his throat and looks back up to Charlie.

'I love her, you know that right?'

'I know you do. She knows that too bud.'

'Then I think it's time we intervene. She needs professional help; this can't go on any longer.'

3

I switch the hair dryer off, leaving it under my dressing table and walk to the kitchen. My freshly dyed hair causes me to take a second look at the reflection of myself in the silver fridge door as I get a bottle of water out to drink. My back pocket vibrates. I pull out my phone and see an unsaved calling me. I let it ring off.

I've had this unsaved number call me non-stop every day for the past two weeks, I want to say it's more than likely one of those scam callers but this time I recognise the number, I'm simply putting off answering it.

'Who was that?' Sebastian emerges from behind me. I look back down at my phone. 'Oh no one, just an unknown number.' As soon as the words leave my mouth my phone rings again, the ringtone echoing throughout the apartment. Before I can grab the phone to decline the call, Sebastian picks up the phone answering it.

'Hello?' He furrows his brow as he gets no response from the caller. 'Who is this?' The line goes dead.

I can feel my body instantly tense up and as soon as he hands the phone back over to me, I relax a little.

'Who was it?' Sebastian looks closely at me, I stop myself from fidgeting.

'I don't know. They hung up. How long have they been calling you?' I slide my phone back into my jean pocket.

'A week or so? I'm sure it's just one of those scam

calls, no need to worry babe.' I kiss him on the forehead and head to my room.

'Kate?' I turn around to look at him. 'You'd tell me, wouldn't you? You know, if anything was bothering you?' If you were in the room, you could probably hear my heart breaking.

'Sebastian, you know I would. Why are you asking?' He moves closer towards me. 'You called me babe. You never call me babe. You hate even being called babe. You're fidgeting, you've dyed your hair and I know you're still having your nightmares.

You've lied to me about that. I just need to know if you're lying to me about anything else.'

I stare at him, slightly astounded but I know I deserved his bluntness. I have been hiding a lot of things from him and I don't need to, he's a grown man, he's stood by my side through everything the past year has bought us. I just feel an overwhelming need to keep him out of this still.

'I'm not lying to you about anything else.' Ironically, I'm lying. 'Why didn't you tell me about the nightmares?'

'I'm sorry. It's just I thought by telling you they'd stopped you'd be able to stop worrying and we could go back to normal and try to build ourselves a normal life again.'

'How can we go back to normal if you just keep lying Kate? I don't know what's going through your head anymore. You're not sleeping, you're barely eating again, you're sneaking off in the middle of the night into the city and not coming back for hours. I know you're in a bad place Kate. I want to help you. I want to love you again.' His voice hitches as he says his last sentence. My heart completely stops.

'You don't love me anymore?' I can't quite get the words out. My whole body goes numb. He leans forward and tries to take my hands in his but I back away.

'I do.'

'Then why did you say that?' 'I will always love you' 'But?'

'At the moment Kate, you're making it so difficult. All I want to do is be there for you, help you with everything and anything, but not telling me what's going on is making it really fucking hard. I lost my job for you. I am willing to move wherever you want in the world so that you are safe. I would die for you, you know that. But it's so fucking hard to love you when you won't open up to me. I don't even know if you want help. I don't even know if you still love me.'

If a year ago, the love of my life had said this to me I would be sobbing my heart out, begging him to stay, telling him I'd change. Deep, deep down I want to do that but up on the surface I'm cold. He's completely right. I've changed, I don't let on but I guess that's what trauma does to you right?

'You know I love you, Sebastian. I couldn't have gotten through the past year without you. You know that.'

'Then show me.' 'What?'

'Show me you love me.' I start fidgeting. 'How?'

'You get help. Charlie and I have spoken, we'll get you checked in at a rehabilitation centre and you'll stick at it, and you come home, and we start fresh, just like we planned.'

'When?'

'As soon as we can get you booked in. There's a place on the Upper East Side, they can accept you from tomorrow afternoon.' 'You've already contacted them?'

'We had to Kate. You can't live like this. You're a shell of yourself. I want to be able to live the best years of our lives with the woman I fell in love with.'

'The way I'm reacting is normal! Would it be normal if I just carried on like nothing had happened. Like I hadn't been taken advantage of by multiple people in multiple ways?' 'No of course not, we both think that you just need to talk to someone. Someone that's not us.' I bow my head down to the ground. I know I'm not going to win this one. 'I'll think about it. Are you coming to visitation with us today?'

'I'll come, but I'll stay in the car, you two should do this together.' I smile at him and nod.

'Alright, I'll carry on getting ready then.' Charlie comes out of his room as I turn around. He looks ready to go already, I frown at his outfit. He smiles at me.

'Don't worry, we're just going to pick up some groceries before we set off, do you need anything?' I shake my head.

'No thanks. What time will you be back?'

'About 12, then we'll leave at half 12. Visitation is booked for 1:30.' Charlie walks towards the front door as he's speaking to me and Sebastian follows. He grabs his keys and they are standing at the front door about to leave.

'Okay, well I'll see you when you get back.' They both leave, Sebastian leaving quickly behind my brother with nothing but a muttered goodbye, shutting the door as they go. The second the door closes my phone begins to ring again. I take it out of my pocket and it vibrates in my hand until I decide to answer to the unsaved number.

'Hello?' Hesitantly, I answer.

'Katheryn?' I recognise his voice instantly and my heart sinks deeper into my chest. I scurry to my bedroom closing and locking my door.

'How did you get my number?' I begin to pace around the king size bed. 'It doesn't matter. I need to see you. It's important. I need help.' I scoff. 'Why should I help you, Harvey? You're a coward.'

'Please.' I roll my eyes leaving the conversation in silence.

'Can you come to my apartment in 10 minutes?'

'I'll be there in 5.' I hang up instantly. Just hearing his voice again causes my hands to clam up. I look down at my hands, seeing the ring Doreen gave me.

Her words still so fresh in my mind as if she spoke them yesterday.

Give him hell Katheryn.

4

A loud bang at the front door knocks me out of my thoughts. I smooth down clothes, pushing my hair behind my ears. I walk over to the door, taking a deep breath in before opening it and there he was. Harvey Fernsby, but perhaps not as I remember him. Long gone were his pristine suits and $800 shoes. His hair was hanging down into his eyes and those eyes were bloodshot with dark bags accompanying them.

I let him in and we stand between the kitchen and the bedrooms, he seems too agitated to sit down.

'Where have you been?' I keep my tone blunt.

'Keeping a low profile, is anyone here?' Harvey keeps looking around to make sure we are alone. His whole personality has changed. It's as if he's snorted grams of cocaine in one sitting.

'No one is here Harvey. Keeping a low profile because you don't want to get caught?'

He looks at me like a little child. He paces closer to me 'I can't go to prison.' He sounds so desperate and it's bringing me too much joy. I laugh at his admission.

'And I can?'

'This isn't what I want!' He snaps back instantly.

'This isn't what anyone wants. YOU! You are the reason we are in this mess. If it wasn't for you, Joe would be alive. If it wasn't for you thinking you had one up on me and telling the police about what happened that night, you wouldn't be on the run. Harvey, you forgot one thing. I am a Simmonds. Simmonds always get what they want. You will pay for everything. I promise you that. You are a coward, just like your father. Always running and hiding, it's over now.'

'I never intended for Joe to get hurt, for anyone to get hurt. Katheryn please! I didn't mean to kill him. You were the one who was holding the gun in the first place. You were the one who was aiming at me, this isn't my fault.'

'You were keeping me hostage in a room after you had spiked my drink and sexually assaulted me. I think you'll find I had every right to threaten you with a gun. You were the one who foolishly tried to tackle it off of me. I tried to save Joe. I shouted at him to get out and I saw him sprinting for the door until you forced your hand over mine and pulled the trigger.

Don't deny it Harvey, you had planned to frame

me this whole time, didn't you? That nice act back at my parent's house, it was all a massive set up.'

Harvey backs away from me, staring me down. 'I just didn't think you'd- '

'What? You didn't think my brother would find the best lawyer in the city to defend me? Money is power Harvey, even you should know that.'

The front door starts to unlock, and I mutter a small 'fuck' under my breath. Harvey looks back and forth repeatedly from the door back to me but by the time he tries to escape the boys have already entered the room. Sebastian walks in first carrying two shopping bags and as soon as he sees Harvey's face, he drops the bags on the floor.

'What the fuck is he doing here?' He charges towards us both. 'Get the fuck away from her!'

Harvey instantly holds his hands up in surrender.

'Woah, woah, It's fine we're just talking.' Sebastian swings for Harvey but Charlie stops him just in time, pulling Sebastian away. I stand back just watching this unfold. Not once in my life have I seen Sebastian this angry.

I look over at Charlie who's calming Sebastian down and he meets my gaze. I keep my gaze cold and try not to let anything on to my brother.

'What's going on?' Charlie directs his question at me, completely bypassing Harvey who's still cowering between us.

'Nothing. He's just leaving.' I reply with no emotion, just simply staring Harvey out.

His eyes plead with me but I don't give in, leaving us four in deafening silence. 'Leave then.' Sebastian shatters the tension.

Harvey cowers past the two men and out of the

door without saying a single word. Once the door closes behind him, Charlie locks it from the inside. Sebastian practically runs over to me engulfing me into a hug, completely forgetting my new boundaries.

'Did he hurt you?' I let him hold me longer than usual but I swiftly move away.

'No, I'm fine.' I can tell from my blunt response that Sebastian is hurt by my attitude.

He stands in front of me looking deeply into my eyes. I try my hardest to reassure him that I'm okay though in the corner of my eye I see Charlie sitting down on the sofa. His arms are crossed and he's just staring me down. I walk over to the kitchen and I start putting some of the groceries away.

'Why was he in our house?'

I don't reply to Charlie. I close the fridge door,

though it slams a little harder than intended. Well, intended slightly.

'What the fuck is going on with you. The past two weeks you have been so fucking shady, not to mention rude. The past few months, I have bent over backwards to get the best lawyers for you, to make sure you're protected, to make sure you don't end up spending the rest of your life in goddamn jail and this is what you do? You let that man into OUR home, knowing full well what he's capable of doing and not only that, completely disrespecting the only two people around you that haven't left your side throughout all of this!' I let my brother's words flow through me. I turn around to face him and see Sebastian giving me the same deep stare while leaning on the kitchen island.

'You want to shout at me too?' Sebastian scoffs and pushes himself up off of the island.

'Charlie has said most of it. He's right. I love you but recently you're testing my limits, Kate. After everything I said to you this morning?' I roll my eyes and he simply stares down at the ground.

'Done?'

As soon as the words enter the atmosphere, Charlie launches from his chair and darts to his room, shaking his head as he goes.

"Don't walk away.' Charlie turns back around, standing next to Sebastian, seconds away from launching another scathing attack on my character.

I reach down my top and pull out an old iPhone from my bra. I dangle it in front of them as if to tease the boys.

'I recorded everything Harvey said while he was here. I have his confession to murdering Joe.' My words are still just as blunt and monotone. Charlie and Sebastian both look at me in disbelief.

'Are you joking?' Charlie asks. 'Nope. It's all here.'

'Can I?' Charlie holds his hand out and I place the phone into his hand. He replays the audio on loudspeaker, Harvey's confession filling the silence in the room. 'I'm calling Maggie right now.' Charlie pulls out his phone to call Maggie and heads straight into his bedroom, shutting the door behind him. I turn to look back at Sebastian and see he's still staring me down, unsure on what to make of what just happened.

'I'm sorry for being a bitch. I do appreciate everything you've done for me. Put it down to stress?' His face begins to soften.

'You do know that as soon as you're officially proven innocent, that excuse is never going to fly?' Sebastian relaxes and I practically jog over to him and engulf him in a hug. I pull away from him slightly.

'Everything you said this morning. You're right. I'm sorry for the past few weeks.

He'd been calling me non-stop, begging me to meet him and it bought back everything.' My words are slightly hushed in a way that's only intended for Sebastian to hear.

'Is that the real reason you've been so shady and why the nightmares are back?' He pushes my hair away from face, tucking it behind my ear. I look back at him, guilt weeping out of my eyes. I begin to nod.

'I think so. I just want to go back to California. Start our new lives, like you said.' My voice cracks slightly.

'Hey. You never have to worry about trying to be stronger than you are. You never need to worry about that with me. It kills me that I can't take away everything that happened to you, but I will be here with you from now on. You're not going through this alone.'

Sebastian pulls me back in, hugging me tightly. I don't pull away, and for the first time in a what feels like eternity, I sink into his arms as if every guard I've had up has shattered into the ground. The moment is ruined as soon as my brother walks out of his bedroom, closing the door and clearing his throat.

'Sorry to interrupt, but we need to leave if we're going to make visitation.' Sebastian and I pull away but he pulls me closer to his side and grabs my hand, squeezing it slightly. Charlie notices and smiles at us before skirting around us, he picks up his coat and stands by the door. Sebastian and I follow and for a second, I feel like a small part of me has stitched it's self back together.

5

Charlie pulls up into the car park of the correctional facility. Eleanor and William are being held there until their trial. For the last few months, the date of each trial keeps getting pushed further and further back. If it's not their lawyer creating some kind of fuss, then it's Eleanor faking some kind of illness to get out of it.

I look down at the digital clock on the dashboard and see that we have about five minutes before we have to be at the side door. I unclip my seatbelt and turn round in the seat and see Sebastian staring back at me. I give him a little smile.

'You ok?' He scoots over to the middle and leans forward. I simply nod my head and turn to Charlie beside me. His gaze is fixated ahead, his hands clutching the steering wheel, his knuckles are almost white.

'Hey.' I place my hand over Charlie's and he softens his grip slightly. He pulls away quickly before I have a chance to talk to him. Charlie clears his throat and almost bolts out of the car, leaving Sebastian and I sitting with confused looks on our faces. I look out the window and see him walking straight to the main door of the facility.

'You don't have to go in if you don't want too.' Sebastian breaks my gaze from Charlie. I look back at him and he seems just as concerned as I do.

'No, it's okay. Stay here. I don't think we'll be that long.' I gesture towards Charlie who's now inside the building. Sebastian just nods back at me. I kiss him on the cheek and make my way into the facility.

I shiver as soon as I set foot through the door, passing the security checks. The walls are white just like those from before. I look around and Charlie is nowhere to be seen. I keep walking and at the end of the corridor I see a prison guard standing in front of a grey door with frosted glass.

'Katheryn Simmonds?' His voice is deep and echoes down the hall.

'Yes.' My voice is quiet and a little shaky. The fear of being here alone and not knowing where my brother is seems to be seeping out through my body language.

'In here.' He uses his head to gesture towards the door behind him. I walk up and he lets me in and there sitting on the far right-hand side of the long metal table is Charlie. His eyes are fixated on the floor and shows no reaction when I walk in, dragging the chair beside him for me to sit down. The guard almost slams the door causing me to jump yet no reaction from my brother. I leave it twenty seconds before I attempt to break the ice.

'You don't have to see them. We can leave and go back home, you know that right?' Charlie looks back at me, staring me dead in the eyes. If looks could kill.

'I'm not leaving. I'm fine.' His tone is stern and before I could respond the lock from the door within the room starts to turn and instantly I could feel my heart race. Charlie adjusts in his seat, his back fully up.

I inhale deeply as the door opens and there they were. Eleanor, free from makeup and dressed in grey sweats, far from her Upper East Side designer collection, with William following her behind, looking about ten years older. They both shuffle into the room, taking their seats opposite us, William not looking at either of us in the eye, but Eleanor clearly scoping us out. The bitch.

'You have twenty minutes.' The prison guard announces and then leaves through the frosted door, locking it and standing outside.

No one says a word. Eleanor leans back in her chair, I look at her and I almost don't recognise her. Her whole attitude is different, as if this is her true self, a backstabbing bitch. Sounds about right. I look over to William, who's still got his head down unable to make any kind of eye contact. I sense to my right that Charlie has clocked on and instantly I know this isn't going to go well.

'Ashamed?' His words shatter the silence and stab William, causing him to immediately look up at him.

He doesn't say a thing. Charlie just laughs. I let out a sigh causing Eleanor to take the next jab.

'Why are you even here Katheryn? You've not come to one of our hearings. You're just living the high life walking around like you've not murdered anyone.' Her words lingered and I was slightly taken aback by the fact there's been previous hearings that I had no idea about. I just raise my eyebrows and laugh.

'I'm not the bad person here. You are Eleanor. I didn't murder anyone.'

'I'm your mother. You do not call me Eleanor!' She leans over the table and scolds me. William raises his hand and pulls Eleanor down back into her seat.

'You're not her mother. You're not mine either. You never were. You took that away from us. We wanted to see you because we thought it might help in clearing the air. I must have been out of my mind to even agree to this.' Charlie comes to my rescue as he sees my leg beginning to bob up and down under the table. Eleanor slouches back down into the chair clearly fuming.

The lock on the frosted door begins to unlock and the prison guard comes back in.

'Sorry to interrupt, Charlie can we speak outside?' Charlie looks back at me. 'You'll be alright?' Charlie's hand on my shoulder reassures me slightly.

'Yeah of course, go.' I lie through my teeth. Charlie leaves and the door locks behind him.

I look back at the two people in front of me and I soon realise I have no feelings towards them. I'm not even angry anymore and if I try hard enough, I'm sure I can convince myself that they never even existed at all. I subconsciously find myself playing with Doreen's ring on my finger. Within seconds my thoughts are broken by Eleanor shouting.

'I WANT TO LEAVE NOW. GET ME OUT OF HERE.' I am truly confused by her behaviour. She is a complete stranger. They both are. William barely flinches at her shouting. The prison guard comes back in and restrains Eleanor. I stand looking at them both.

'No one likes a mad woman, Eleanor.' I turn my back before she can even reply, leaving the room I walk back down the empty white corridor.

I turn into the waiting room expecting to see Charlie but I'm welcomed to another empty room. I turn back around, and no one is around. I make my way back out of the facility and walk back to the car expecting him to be there instead, but it's just Sebastian. I open the car door and get in.

'How did it go?' Sebastian's words were gentle, I turn around to look at him, my eyes frowning with worry.

'Has Charlie been here?' He automatically can see the panic coursing through my body.

'No. What's happened?'

'It didn't go well. The guard came back in the room and asked to speak to Charlie alone, I just thought he'd come back here?'

'No, I haven't seen anyone leave the building apart from you.'

'What if somethings happened Sebastian?' Suddenly the air around me becomes harder to get into my lungs.

'Hey, it's alright. I'm here. Sebastian leans forward from the back seat and cups his hands around my face. 'Just breathe, I'm sure it's all okay.' I close my eyes and focus on my breathing until the car door opening startles me.

Charlie comes bounding into the car, his body hitting the back of the seat jolting the car slightly.

'Where have you been, are you ok?' Charlie's eyes are bloodshot, a trait I've not yet seen on him.

'Maggie was there. She wanted to talk to me about some stuff.' He clears his throat, still a terrible liar.

'Charlie.' He looks at me bluntly. The sadness in his eyes changes to remorse. 'They've found a body.'

6

Before I could even react to the bombshell that Charlie dropped, we were speeding down FDR Drive making a beeline back to my apartment. Every time I tried to even think of something to say, my mouth would open and I would be immediately cut off.

'Kate. Not now. Just wait till we get home. Please.' I sigh, running my hand over my face.

'Just tell me who's body it is! Is it Joe's?' Charlie doesn't answer me but instead just pushes his foot further to the ground causing us to almost glide back into Brooklyn.

We park up abruptly and one by one pile back into the apartment. Dropping the keys onto the counter, Charlie sits in the armchair, his elbows leaning on his legs, his hands supporting his head. I sit down opposite him on the sofa, Sebastian taking his seat next to me. Charlie exhales.

'Maggie is going to meet us here in an hour or so.' Those words are not what I wanted to hear.

'Whose body is it, Charlie?' He looks at me again with those sad eyes. He darts them over to Sebastian and in the corner of my eye I can see my boyfriend nodding slightly back at my brother.

'It's not Joe's.' Some relief evaporates from my body but Sebastian's grip on my thigh is telling me to not be so sure. Charlie shuffles in his seat.

'Remember they did a search at William and Eleanor's house? They found a bunch of documents and old invoices, anyway, among that they found all these documents for the Hamptons summer house. Documents that showed they had extensive works done the same year I allegedly disappeared.' I glance over at Sebastian who's now looking back at me displaying the same look as Charlie.

'Can you just say it instead of you both staring at me with those sad eyes!' 'Kate, they found the remains of a body underneath the pool. They think it's Jones's.' 'Hold on. You're telling me Jones's body was buried under the pool?'

'That's what they're thinking. They have to run DNA tests on the bones and everything else but it's very likely that it's her.'

'Very likely? What do you mean?'

'It was done within 24 hours of her dying. Her

body was preserved by the concrete.' Even Charlie's voice breaks.

'The pool I learned to swim in? The pool I used to try to swim to the bottom of and ouch the ground, this whole time my mother was buried beneath it?' Charlie's eyes fill up with tears as my voice breaks.

I look to the side of me and see Sebastian staring back with a sympathetic look on his face. I sink my body into the plump cushions of the sofa and exhale expecting the weight of the news to evaporate from my body, but it doesn't, it just stays with me, pushing me further back into the sofa. I find myself subconsciously twirling the ring on my finger round and round, almost as if I'm in a state of panic, yet my mind is completely numb and switched off. A loud knock echoes through the silent apartment and makes us all jump. Sebastian stands to open the door. I hear a familiar voice, but I don't turn to see who it is until I see their body walk in, pulling up a chair in front of me.

Her perfectly straight grey hair graces the tops of her shoulders, barely touching the beige cashmere coat that covers her body. I look up and see Maggie sitting in front of me. Her thick black glasses frame her face. It's not until she reaches out and holds my hands to stop me from spinning the ruby ring on my finger that I hear what she's saying. 'Katheryn? You understand, don't you?' Maggie's voice is a little raspy and the somewhat thick New York accent makes you feel completely comfortable in her presence. I clear my throat and sit forward.

'No. No I don't. Can you say again?' Charlie and Sebastian are standing behind her, Charlie begins to walk forward but Maggie holds her hand out to stop him. She learns further forward into her chair, clutching my hands a little tighter and it was only then that I realise I'm shaking.

'We need to take some DNA from you. Charlie is going to have to do this too. It'll help us confirm whose body it is, ok?'

'Ok. That's fine. Do whatever you need Maggie.' My voice is quiet but strong.

She turns around and nods at Charlie before getting up and walking to the kitchen with him. Simultaneously, Sebastian joins me on the sofa.

'Come here.' He pulls me into his side and he plants a kiss onto my head.

'I just want this to be over Sebastian. I just feel exhausted and as much as finding Charlie was great and I get to have him in my life again, I do sometimes wish I never even bothered.'

'I know, but this will be over soon, I promise you.

You've made it through the worst of it, remember that.' I move away and look up at him, kissing him on the lips. Charlie and Maggie come over and Sebastian and I both stand up. Maggie has my old iPhone in her hand along with some swabs in tubes.

'Good work Katheryn. This is extremely damming. From all that I've heard of the recording, it's definitely going to send him down.' I raise my eyebrows 'You mean that? Like, I won't get sentenced at all?'

'I can't promise anything Katheryn, but you know I will try my best.' I nod in agreement, my hopes come back down to earth. 'Now, I just need to take a swab of the inside of your mouth, just like I did with Charlie a second ago.' I nod my head. Maggie opens a tube and pulls out the swab. I open my mouth and she does what she needs until she places the swab back into the tube and drops it into a clear bag along with Charlie's.

'All done. I'm dropping these off on my way back tonight. As soon as I get any kind of update, I'll let you know. Get some rest.' Maggie looks me dead in the eyes before she picks up her large leather tote bag and heads for the door. Charlie thanks her and escorts her out of our apartment. As soon as he's out of ear shot, I turn to Sebastian.

'Do you mind if I just have some time alone?' He almost looks disheartened, but he knows I need my space sometimes.

'Of course. Just let me know if you need me.' We kiss once more and I head into our bedroom, locking the door behind me.

After the search of our family home, some of the items they found were released to us after they had been searched through for evidence. Charlie and I were given the photo albums, everything else is being put into storage. I pull out a large box from under my bed, just the same as the one I kept all of my own evidence in from when I was trying to find Charlie.

However, in this one is album upon album of photos. I open the first leather bound album and the first picture I see is a family portrait taken in the garden of the Hamptons house. I must have been about one. I've got a god awful white and pink sundress on and bless Charlie he's wearing golfing attire.

I continue flicking through the pages and notice the further I make my way through the book, the more candid the photos become. As if what Eleanor thought were the worst photos have been hidden away at the back. I come across one photo that makes my heart sink. Nanny Jones, and Charlie sitting on the grass next to the pool, all playing building blocks with me.

You can see the genuine happiness radiating from

Jones' smile and it's only in that second, I begin to see our similarities. I pull out another album, one from my senior prom and I begin to compare Jones and I. We definitely have the same nose and now with my darker hair it seems I may be my mother's twin. I grab all of the photos I could find of Jones and head back out into the living room. The boys just stay watching some kind of sport, sprawled on the sofa.

'Do we know Jones' first name?' Charlie looks startled but relaxes slightly as he adjusts in his seat.

'No, I never did, I just knew her has Nanny Jones. We might be able to find out after the DNA test?' They'll probably have records of her birth certificate somewhere. You alright?' I walk over and sit in between both of the boys, showing them the photos I found.

'Yeah, I've just been looking through some old photos and I can't get over how similar Jones and I look.' Sebastian grabs one out of my hand almost immediately.

'Woah. You're identical!' Charlie leans over and grabs another one out of my lap.

'I'd never noticed this before! Now you have darker hair I can definitely see it.' I look up at him.

'You know even though you look like William, you've definitely got her eyes.' Charlie nudges me affectionately.

'Her name might be listed on your birth certificates. Do you have a copy of those?' Sebastian adds to the conversation.

'I don't have mine, do you Charlie?'

'Nope. I think maybe it's with all the documents that are being searched through.' Sebastian sits up and looks at us both.

'How have you managed to get through life without having a copy of your birth certificate?'

'Well, Eleanor and William sorted most things out for me, like my bank account was set up for me when I was a child.'

'But what about when you bought this place? Surely you needed ID as proof of identity?'

'I paid for the apartment in cash remember? You helped me with the transfer. I had my driver's license, no one asked for my birth certificate.' Sebastian raises his eyebrows almost in disbelief.

'Similar with me actually, though I'm renting my home from Doreen.'

'They really had you wrapped around their finger didn't they.' Sebastian just stares at me as if he's looking for me to agree with him, which to some extent I do, but the words still sting a little.

'I don't know what you want me to say Sebastian. You know this, you knew this from the very moment we met.' My words come out more defensive than I intended.

'I'm sorry, but sometimes when I hear things like this, I just can't believe the shit that they did. To both of you. It's fucked up!'

'At least they're getting what they deserve now, that's the main thing.' Charlie tries to calm the air as I sit there in silence, the sting of Sebastian's words is still buzzing around my body.

Sometimes it catches me off guard and sometimes when someone else points out something I'm intentionally ignoring to try to get over, it knocks me for six. As much as I agree with Charlie that, yes, they've been arrested for their crimes and hopefully will be sentenced, I truly hate how I've let myself live in that world for so long. If only I could've broken from them sooner, if only Charlie hadn't had to run away. If only. Hindsight is a bitch.

7

In the past two days since we had the swab tests, whenever Charlie's phone rings my heart has jumped out of my chest and every time it does, it's always a false alarm. Even the sound of someone else's phone ringing in the supermarket puts me on edge.

'Kate? Katheryn?' It's not until I feel Sebastian's hand on my arm that he manages to get my attention. I blink at him with a confused expression on my face.

'I was just asking if we needed anymore coffee...are you ok?' I shake my head as if to shake the thoughts in my head away.

'Yes, sorry. We do.' Sebastian looks at me, not believing at all that I'm alright but he picks up some coffee from the shelf and places it in the trolley.

'Your knuckles are white.' 'Huh?'

Sebastian points down at my hands clutching the handle of the shopping cart. 'You've been zoning out and holding on so tightly to the trolley, are you having a panic attack?' I look down and I haven't even noticed until he pointed it out. I slowly loosen my grip.

'No, no, I'm fine. I'm just tired. Promise.' I smile at him reassuringly but he still doesn't buy it.

The journey from the checkout to the car and back home again was comfortably peaceful. We managed to get back and put all our groceries away without one mention of my mental state. I make us some lunch and we end up sitting on the sofa together watching a Disney film, just like old times. Half-way through the film, Charlie comes home. He swings the front door open and heads straight to his room, locking the door as he closes it behind him. Sebastian and I stare at each other.

'He's had the call, hasn't he?' I immediately tense up. I go to stand up but Sebastian stops me.

'Hey, just give him time. It's his mother too.' I lean back into the sofa and try to give the film my full attention but to no avail.

It took Charlie exactly one hour and fifty-four minutes before he came out of his room.

One hour and fifty-four minutes of excruciating anticipation for me. Except the anticipation was met with confusion as when Charlie came out of his room, he simply left the apartment in a puff of smoke without one single word. Something isn't right. How bad must the news have been? What is the worst situation in this scenario? My mind doesn't stop going over itself until he returns and even then, it barely slows down.

Sebastian and I haven't moved from the sofa when Charlie returns. He strolls in and hovers over us.

'Seb, can I have a word? In private?' I look frantically back and forth between the two men.

'Uh yeah, of course bud.' They both go into Charlie's room and leave me sat in silence.

I don't even try to listen at the door, I switch the tv over and find something mundane to watch and within 20 minutes the two men both emerge back into the living room. I look at them both and painted among their faces are the looks of sympathy. I choose to simply ignore it and carry on watching the TV. Petty, I know.

The evening plays out just like any other evening. Not one person in the apartment has let on to anything that happened earlier in the day, and I won't be the one to push for the information. My limits are tested when I wake up to get some water in the middle of the night and find Sebastian and Charlie whispering in the kitchen.

'Are you going to actually tell me what's going on or do I have to play dumb until you do.' My words seem to cut through the tension surrounding us.

'Kate, trust me, just give him time.' Sebastian saunters over and tries to calm me down.

'No Sebastian! Why are you in on this?'

'Katheryn, don't act like a spoilt girl, I'm trying to help you, to protect you, just leave it. At least for a few days, ok? Let me sort this.' Charlie is clearly agitated. He runs his hands over his face, rubbing his eyes.

'Protect me? Charlie, please! I can handle it! What's the problem?'

'KATHERYN HOW MANY TIMES! LET IT GO!' Charlie's voice rattles the whole apartment, even making Sebastian jump. His outburst causes a lump in my throat to appear. I don't retaliate, I just simply walk back into my bedroom.

Half an hour later, I feel the right-hand side of the bed dip down and my boyfriend's hands snake around my waist pulling me closer. I pretend to be asleep and it fools him. I lay for two hours beside him and as soon as I'm content in knowing he's fully asleep, I sneak out of bed and tip toe back into the kitchen.

I never used to be like this. I never used to sneak, and if I did, it would only be out of the house to go to a party. I never used to purposely sneak around to find out information on anyone. Hell, I never used to kill anyone either, but here we are.

I find Charlie's jacket and check through the

pockets for his phone in the hopes he would have left it out here, but nothing. I check the living room and down the sides of the sofa. I start to walk back to my room when a flash of potential stupidity crosses my mind.

I reach out and slowly turn the door handle to Charlie's room and there he is. Asleep in the king size bed. I tiptoe to his side of the bed and find his phone sitting on the table beside him. I attempt to unlock it with using his birthday and bingo. I try to stay as still as possible as he moves in his sleep. I frantically scroll through his texts and email looking for anything to help me out, and that's when I saw it. An email titled 'DNA Results' and perhaps I gasped a little too loudly in potential celebration because as I looked up Charlie's eyes were staring right back at me.

'What are you doing?' His voice was quiet, calm

and raspy but furious all at the same time. I just stare him out in complete shock as if there was no chance of him waking up. I'm an idiot. I try to get words out but I just stutter. I slowly place his phone back down on the table and back away slightly.

'I couldn't sleep- '

'So, you decided to go through my phone?' Charlie sits up in his bed pulling the duvet up with him to cover his naked chest. He reaches over and puts the side lamp on, and it just emphasises the fact that I'm a deer caught in headlights.

'No!'

'No? You're a shit liar Katheryn. Why don't you trust me? Why can't you just let this lie. Just for a few days, for my sake?' His voice starts to hitch, and I can't tell if it's because he's tired or if he's about to cry. 'I do trust you!'

'No, you don't Katheryn. Otherwise, you wouldn't have crept into my room and started going through my phone!'

'Charlie, I'm sorry.'

'No, you're not. I understand you've been through some fucking terrible shit and I sympathise I really do. I hate that you went through all of that just to find me and it kills me to know that I couldn't protect you all those years, but I need you to just trust me when I say this is for your own good. You are becoming your own worst enemy. Just let me protect you now. Please.' We end up just looking at each other with tears in our eyes. Why do I always feel a need to control everything and everyone around me? Maybe it's because I don't feel in control of myself. Maybe if I can make sure everything around me is ok and I'll be ok in the end and maybe I'll be able to sleep.

'Can I ask you two things and then I'll go.' My voice barely makes a sound. Charlie simply nods his head at me.

'Go on.'

'Was it her body under the pool?' 'Yes.' 'Is she for certain our mother?' 'Yes.'

There's something about Charlie's eyes looking back at me that breaks my fucking heart. I know there's more to this than he's telling me, but I'll let him protect me, as he wants, for now.

8

I wake up the next morning and the apartment is eerily quiet. I turn to my right and notice a note on Sebastian's pillow.

'Gone out with Charlie, we'll be back this afternoon. S x'

I turn back to my side of the bed and see that it's only 9am. My suspicions grow but I try to distract myself by jumping out of bed to do some yoga. Whoever said yoga was a helpful distraction was wrong. All that it's done is just made me be anxious and paranoid while looking like an idiot with my legs up in the air in hopes that I'll be more centered with the world. I call bullshit.

A couple of hours pass, and I decide to give Sebastian a call, but it goes to voicemail.

Twice. The longer I don't hear from either of them the more agitated I get. So, this is what trauma does to you. I find myself constantly moving from one seat to another and when I do finally get comfortable, my leg doesn't stop bobbing up and down as Charlie's words continue to hammer around my head. I start playing with my hair and my hand gets caught. I start to untangle my hand from my hair and realise it's Doreen's ring that's caught in my hair.

I take it off and stare at it. I miss her. I miss her warmth, her acceptance, her listening to me without judgement. I wonder if she's okay. I wonder if she knows that Frank is actually my brother and that Frank isn't actually Frank. I wonder if she heard on the news about my family. I wonder who else she has helped in the time that she helped me. I pull my laptop from the coffee table in front of me and decide to search all the possible words that would be able to find her motel. I never got the name, in fact I never recall seeing a sign stating the name, just a dusty car park and a flashing vacancy sign was all that I remember.

Sunset Valley Motel. There was no active website but there was a trip adviser account with a phone number. That'll do. The phone rings three times before it's answered and the voice on the end of the phone instantly brings me to tears. I choke on my words before I can even get them out.

'Sunset Valley Motel, how can I help?'

'Doreen?' My voice hitches and I hear her gasp slightly.

'Katheryn is that you?' I cover my mouth to stop myself from sobbing. Hearing her voice again has opened up a valve in me that needed to be released.

'It's me. I just wanted to say 'Hi'.'

'Oh, darling girl. I've been so worried about you. I've prayed for you every day since I met you.' I already feel so much calmer just hearing her southern dulcet tones. I relax into the armchair.

'So much has happened. I can't even put it into words.'

'You don't need to sweetheart. As long as you're safe now. Are you back home now?' 'I am. I'm in New York. I'm living with my boyfriend and my brother. I found him Doreen!' She chuckles down the phone. Her laugh is husky and almost vibrates down the line. 'I know you did sweetheart. See the thing is darlin', Charlie called me just before you headed back to New

York, explaining everything. Everything from the moment that he turned up to my door to the moment I met you.'

'You know everything?'

'Yes, darlin' and it's okay.' A whole ton of weight seems to shift off of my body and disintegrate into the air and as soon as it does, I can feel a sea of tears fall down my face.

'I'm so sorry.' I managed to get out those three words as I sob down the phone.

'You have nothing to apologise for Katheryn. I do need to tell you I'm coming into the city though. I've been called up to give a statement against Harvey Fernsby. Now I don't have to do it if you don't want me too, I will only do what you're comfortable with, it's up to you.' I try my best to dry my face.

'I haven't even been told there was going to be a trial against him.'

'They only contacted me yesterday afternoon, maybe they're contacting your brother. They've provisionally booked the trial next week.'

'Oh. Well, sure. If they've asked you to give a statement, then of course.'

'Alright darlin'. I'll see you soon then. I've got to go but please call me anytime, don't be a stranger.'

'Bye Doreen, thank you.'

We both hang up the phone simultaneously and right on cue the front door opens. I rush to stand up and make a beeline for my room, with hopes neither of them didn't see my face, I close the door behind me making sure I lock it as I go.

I sit down at my dressing table and use face wipes to remove the sadness traced on my skin. The bedroom door handle rattles as I add the moisturiser to my skin and after the second attempt the person on the other side of the door stops and walks away.

Hearing Doreen's voice again made me feel better and worse at the same time. It's almost like I'm constantly chasing echoes just to get back to what was before, yet what was before was just more pain as if it would cancel out the pain, I'm in now. Doreen brings me comfort and hope but also just transports back to a time of pure danger and I can't seem to find that line to separate it all.

Is that something I'm just going to have to get used too? Being reminded on the daily of everything that happened. Having to walk on eggshells for the rest of my life just in case I get triggered? Having the ones closest to me wrap me in cotton wool so I just don't get hurt again. Can I survive this?

9

I bundled myself up into a ball and tucked the duvet around me. The intensity of the crying had knocked me for six. I manage to doze off for at least half an hour before the vibration of my phone on the bedside table wakes me. Sebastian. I answer it and before I could say hello, he talks first.

'Hello you. You alright?'

'Why are you calling me? You're literally in the next room!' He scoffs down the phone.

'Well, someone locked themselves in their room, didn't they?' I sit up and see the door locked in front of me, and I instantly remember everything, causing my stomach to flip. I get up and saunter over to unlock the door, leaving it slightly ajar. I scramble back into bed.

'It's open now. You can come in.'

'You sure? You can have some more alone time if you want?'

'No, I want to see you, can we cuddle for a bit?' The phone line goes dead, and I look up to the doorway and see Sebastian standing there, leaning against the door frame in a black button down shirt and black tailored trousers. His multi-coloured spotty socks standing out especially.

'Of course we can.' He comes and lays next to me as I cuddle into his chest, laying in content silence.

'I called Doreen today.' My words are softly spoken and Sebastian doesn't flinch. He simply just keeps running his hand up and down the top of my arm.

'You did? Is she ok?' His questions are hushed.

'She's good. It was good to speak to her. I had a bit of a cry. She said she's been asked to come to the city to be a part of Harvey's trial. You'll get to meet her.' He squeezes me a little tighter.

'I could tell you had but I didn't want to push, are you feeling a bit better?' Sebastian ignores the main part of what I just said which indicates to me that he already knew. I sigh, loudly.

'Yeah, better now.' I immediately switch off from the conversation. The feeling of everyone knowing something that I don't truly disheartens me. Does this make me a narcissist? Am I being a spoilt brat?

We end up falling asleep and are awoken by the smell of hot food filling the apartment.

I grab an old sweater and some old joggers pulling them onto my body and follow Sebastian out into the kitchen. Charlie is stood there, behind him is a fully set out table with serving bowls full of potatoes, vegetables with melted butter and slices of roast beef.

'Hungry?' Charlie addresses the room, and a resounding "Yes" is echoed into the apartment. We swarm to the table, and each take a seat, Charlie serves us each before sitting down himself and tucking in.

'What's the occasion?' I take a bite of potato and the butter just melts in my mouth.

'Well, there isn't really one, but I thought I'd do something nice and we need a chat. All of us, together.' My heart drops and it's written all over my face.

'It's alright.' Sebastian reaches over and holds my hand in his. I look at him with worry in my eyes.

'I'm sorry if you feel a bit ambushed but I wanted to do this to make it easier for you.' 'It's okay Charlie, I appreciate it.'

He smiles back at me and puts his cutlery down on the table despite barely touching his meal.

'You know that it was her body in the pool and you know the DNA test came back positive for being our mother.' I nod my head and Sebastian's grip gets a little tighter on my hand.

'Okay...' I try to fill the silence in the gaps that Charlie leaves.

'So today, Sebastian and I went to meet Maggie. They completed a post-mortem and found her birth records on system. Her full name is Louisa Jones.' I try to swallow away my anxiety, but it doesn't seem to go away. I clear my throat and Charlie continues.

'The thing is I've known this for a couple of days. The reason we saw Maggie today is that, alongside the birth records on the system, they found some other records, official documents actually, that matched up with documents they found at Dad's house.' Each word that Charlie says becomes slower.

'Okay Charlie, none of this is making sense, get to the point.' He inhales deeply. 'Louisa was 34 when she died.' I look at both of them staring back at me waiting for the penny to drop, but it didn't.

'So?' Charlie's brows furrow slightly, almost looking sympathetically at me. 'It means she only turned 18 two months before I was born.' If you listen close enough, you'd be able to hear the penny finally drop. I let go of Sebastian's hand and push my hair behind my ears, leaning forward in my chair. 'Does that mean Dad...?' Charlie just nods his head.

'The thing is, these documents we came across were two Affidavits. Both are statements from Louisa; however, one is admission to Dad forcing himself on her and the second is a completely different story. Only the second one is recorded on the police systems.'

I sit back in the chair and zone out. The first thing that comes to mind is, why would she change her story? But the thing is, I'm not in much of a situation to say that. To this day, Sebastian still doesn't know the full extent of what happened between Harvey and I in Vegas. Like Charlie said back when he told me everything, too much money holds way too much power.

'He paid her to change her story, didn't he?' My words were quiet but still managed to echo through the room.

'We don't have the proof yet but it's more than likely.' I just nod.

'I'm assuming you know about the trial against Harvey?' Charlie just drops his head as if he's been caught out.

'Yeah, Maggie called me yesterday to let me know the evidence you sent in has been accepted. I wanted to tell you this first.'

'It's okay. I spoke to Doreen earlier. She's coming into town to give her statement at the trial. Is there a date?'

'It'll be nice to see her.' He stutters slightly causing me to raise my eyebrows. 'In two weeks.' Everything Charlie is saying seems as if he's just talking to keep the peace. I push my dinner plate away from me and stand up from the table.

'I'm going to go for a walk, I need some air.' Charlie just nods at me.

'Do you want to go alone?' Sebastian speaks for the first time. I just stare back at him.

'Actually, I'd like it if we could go together, if that's

okay.' He beams at me. 'Of course. Let me get my shoes on.'

10

The sun was slowly setting across the Brooklyn skyline as Sebastian and I strolled through Brig Park. We sit down on the concrete steps overlooking the East River.

'I know it's a stupid question, but are you ok?' I look to my right and he's staring at me. Not inquisitively, not like he's wanting to get information out of me but just lovingly. His eyes are almost like pools of comfort, just waiting for me to dive in. I inhale deeply.

'Honestly? This is a lot. Like, I just feel a bit overwhelmed. I don't mean to shut you out at all, I'm just so tired Seb.' My voice begins to crack.

'Come here.' He pulls my into his side as I just sob into his chest.

'I hate that I don't tell you everything and I let it eat me up inside. I want to spend the rest of my life with you and I don't understand how you're still here taking my shit. I never really told you what happened between Harvey and I and now everything with Louisa and what Charlie told me tonight, I just feel like history is repeating itself and I don't want that to happen. Finding everything out about my so called family has made me feel like I don't know who I am. My father raped my biological mother. She was seventeen and he decided to throw money at her to keep her quiet and then thirteen years later, no doubt, the same thing happened again. It makes me not want to be here anymore Sebastian.' He doesn't reply, he just holds me a little tighter.

'You don't have to tell me anything. Wait until you're ready.' I pull away slightly and look back at him.

'I don't think I ever will be ready. I want to be honest with you.' I look around and it's only us and the sea. Sebastian reassuringly nods.

'I only want to ask one question and then you can do all the talking.' 'Okay?'

'That scar on your stomach. How did you get that?' I frown at him. 'You know that.' 'No, I don't Kate. When we were in California at Charlie's place, the night I arrived I saw you covered in bruises and a dressing over your wound, but I never asked how.'

I frown at him a little harder, sure that I did tell him but the more I think about it the more unsure I'm becoming.

'In Vegas at the hotel. Harvey and I got into a fight. He tried to pressure me into giving him information.

He spiked my drink, and he was up in my face, so I smashed my glass over his head to get him off me. He fell to the floor, so I tried to get away from him, but he grabbed my ankle and I fell into the glass coffee table and some glass went into my stomach.'

'That's a big scar for just some glass.' I ignore his comment and continue.

'He got on top of me and pushed me further into the glass. I somehow managed to get away from him and made it back to the bed and that's where I got the gun out.' Sebastian nods again.

I look back out over the sea, not taking my eyes from the waves slowly crashing against the rocks.

'Back when I arrived in Vegas, when I first met Harvey, we got into his car. He had a chauffeur. We were both sitting in the back, and I was so exhausted, so I closed my eyes. He must have thought I was asleep and that's when he sexually assaulted me.' I refuse to look back at Sebastian, but I can instantly tell his whole demeanor has changed. It's tense and as much as I don't want to keep telling the story I feel I must.

'He started rubbing my leg and got closer to me, his body was almost on top of me and his hand crept higher and higher up my thigh. I couldn't bear to open my eyes, he was whispering in my ear, telling me not to worry and I just wanted to cry. I moved further away from him, as much as I could and I was pressed up against the car door, I pushed him off and he shouted at me, something about being ungrateful and he pushed me back holding me down by my shoulders and the next thing I knew, we were at the hotel, and he was acting as if nothing had happened. I just got into the lift and that's when I texted you to say I was in Vegas.' Just like that everything that I wanted to say just started spilling out. Sebastian's body language didn't change much, just became even more tense, if that was possible 'So, when you texted me to tell me you had arrived in Vegas and that you were fine but exhausted, in reality he had just forced himself on you?' I finally look at him and raise my eyebrows slightly just to confirm the truth he was dreading and for a second, I can see tears forming in the wells of his blue eyes.

He reaches his hand out to place on my leg and he almost flinches and looks up at me for consent. I simply take his hand in mine, clutching it.

'It's okay.'

'I knew something had happened, though I did start thinking that maybe you didn't love me anymore or something. You've not let me near you since and when you do, you flinch or walk away but I completely understand now. Whatever it takes for you to heal, I'm here for you.'

'It's not going to be an overnight thing. Some days I feel like myself again and others it's all I can think about and then it crosses my mind that what if it never gets better, what if I'm just on this rollercoaster for the rest of my life? What if I can't get off and it's just going round and round? What do I do then?' The panic in my voice rises.

'Hey. I will be next to you on that rollercoaster. You're not going through this alone, I promise you. However long it takes, even if you feel like you don't ever want to be intimate again, then that's okay too. You've got me for life, no matter what.'

I lean my head onto his shoulder, squeezing his hand a little tighter than before. A few tears trickle down the side of my face, absorbing into his shirt. We sit in silence watching the sea in front of us.

'I'm scared.' My voice comes out shaky and unsure.

'I know you are.'

'I'm scared of everything. I feel like I'm constantly in a state of panic. I'm defensive about everything and everyone. I feel like I'm under attack all of the time. I can't stop thinking about the trial. What if he spins some lines and gets off and I end up going to prison? I'll serve my time, but I don't think I'll be able to survive it. Harvey told me at the beginning of this, that all this chaos was just going to follow me, and he's so right. Even if he does get sentenced and my name is cleared somehow, I still don't believe I can survive it. It makes me so uncomfortable how similar my life got compared to Louisa's. What if Harvey did rape me? What if he got me pregnant? Was he just going to throw money at me? Is he just going to throw money at me now to keep quiet about him sexually assaulting me?'

'If he does then we'll deal with it when it happens. I don't know how I can make you feel better or just not let you have all of this sitting on your shoulders.'

'I don't think anyone can do anything. You being here is enough though. It's just my head.'

'Maybe we should look into that therapist Charlie was talking about. It may help.'

'Do I need to make a decision now?' I look up at him.

'No not at all, just think about it.' I lay my head back down on his shoulder. 'Can I ask one thing?'

'Anything.'

'Did Charlie tell you they'd been previous hearings

for William and Eleanor's case?' His eyes told me everything I needed to know.

'Yeah. He didn't want to add any more stress to you. He didn't want to go to them if you thought he was going behind your back, he hasn't been to any of them. Maggie has been keeping him up to date throughout.' I sigh and stare back out to the sea.

'What're they pleading?'

'Not guilty. Though from the sounds of it, they won't be getting that verdict. There's way too much evidence against them.' I exhale even heavier this time, trying to expel the anxiety filling my body. I lay my head down onto Sebastian's shoulder without a single word. We stay sitting by the sea for another twenty minutes before we silently agree to get up and walk home.

11

As soon as Sebastian and I got home Charlie announced he had rented us all a cabin in Adirondack Park and we spent the weekend in peace surrounded by the mountains. We went hiking and the boys attempted to get me to try fishing and I laughed so hard at one point hot chocolate came out of my nose. It was finally like everything was normal again. We all got everything out in the open, everyone knew everything. The weekend flew by way too quickly and before I knew it, I was sitting back in my apartment watching Charlie pace around the kitchen island.

He eventually stopped moving and sat down on

one of the stools, his back to me, and all I could see was his head dropping and his free hand simply just placed over his face. He hung up the phone and stayed in that position for a good few minutes before I decided to go and comfort him.

I walked over and now both of his hands were cradling his head. I reached my hand out and placed it on his shoulder. He shrugged it off. I gave it a few seconds before I reached out again and placed my hands on top of his. He slapped them away almost instantly.

'Charlie.' My tone is hushed but strained.

'Not now.' He looks up at me and he has tears in his eyes. Though he's looking at me angrily. I turn away from him and open the fridge.

'You know one thing I do remember is that whenever I was sad or I'd have a tantrum, Nanny Jones, sorry, Louisa, would make me a grilled cheese.'

'Don't' Charlie growls making me jump. Clutching the loaf of bread that's in my hands I turn around to face him.

'What?'

'Don't you dare start talking like you knew her! You were three when she died, how could you possibly know anything?' Charlie stands, he somehow seems taller now he's angry, he towers over me and just put the bread on the side.

'I didn't mean to make you feel worse Charlie, I just wanted to help.' No matter what I say it seems to just be making him angrier. He starts to fidget and then looks straight at me.

'You know, I'm glad you don't have a recollection. I'm glad you can't remember the look on her face as she sank beneath the water gasping for air. I'm glad that the image of her sinking to the bottom of the pool doesn't keep you up at night. You know, last year you asked me if I regretted you coming to find me? Well right now, I wish you didn't.' With that final blow he stormed out of the apartment grabbing his coat and keys as he went, slamming the door for one final show of anger. I simply took the bread off the counter and put it back in the fridge. I sit myself down on the sofa and turn the TV on, making a beeline straight to Netflix and putting Friends on. I just stare at the screen not really taking any notice of what's playing in front of me.

The front door unlocks, and I don't take any notice until Sebastian starts talking as soon as he enters. He's always chirpy after he's been to the gym.

'Just passed Charlie on the street, he walked straight past me, didn't say a word, looked mad as hell, is everything alright?' I don't look away from the TV.

'Yeah, he's fine. Had a phone call, then he left.' Sebastian walks over and plonks himself next to me on the sofa, wrapping his arm around my shoulders, completely oblivious. 'Didn't we watch this one the other day?'

'Did we?' Sebastian pulls away slightly and I can feel his gaze on me. He leans forward and pauses the TV.

'Have you two had an argument?' I sigh.

'It was more of Charlie shouting at me than it was an argument.' 'What happened?' Sebastian gets a little defensive.

'No, no, don't, it was my fault, I started talking about Louisa and I shouldn't have. He was on the phone and was pacing and looked upset so I started making a grilled cheese and thought maybe it would help but I barely got the bread out before he flipped at me and told me he wished I never found him, amongst other things. Really it's fine.' I look at Sebastian and smile. Not convincingly but I still smile.

'I'm sure he didn't mean it.' I laugh a little.

'You don't have to justify it, it's alright.' He places a kiss on my forehead before my phone begins to ring, breaking us apart. An unknown number.

'Hello?'

'Katheryn?' I instantly recognise the voice. 'Doreen?'

'Darling my phone's died and I'm using a phone at the hotel. I'm in the city! It's so fancy, I'm like a fish out of water.' I instantly sit up with excitement.

'Where are you staying? I can come and see you!'

'That would be lovely, there's a lovely restaurant in the hotel, we can get lunch? I'm staying at the Stewart Hotel.'

'Seventh avenue in Chelsea, right?'

'That's the one sweetheart.' I look up at the clock above me.

'I can be there in half an hour?' 'Perfect! I'll meet you in the lobby.'

'I can't wait, I'll see you there!' We both hang up the phone and I immediately turn to Sebastian. My eyes wide with excitement, my mood changed instantly.

'That was Doreen, she's in the city, I'm going to meet her for lunch, do you want to come?' He looks at me sweetly.

'I'd love too but you go have a girls' lunch, you deserve it.'

'Ok. I've got to change.' I jog into my bedroom and open the wardrobe. I want to look my best. I pull out a black and white polka dot dress and pair it with a denim jacket and a black cross body bag. I slip on my

Vans and grab my phone and purse, stuffing them in my bag. I walk out applying a little red lipstick as I go and pushing my hair behind my ears.

'This ok?' Sebastian stands up in front of me.

'You look beautiful.' I lean in and kiss him on the cheek.

'I got to go! Will you be able to let me in? I can't find my keys!'

'Of course, go and have fun!' I almost sprint out of the apartment and I'm too excited to even wait for the elevator, so I hurry down the stairs and out of the front door, hailing the first cab I see.

Pulling up outside the hotel I check my makeup one last time and hop out. I stand outside the hotel doors for a second and take a deep breath. I look through the glass from where I'm standing, and I'm instantaneously transported back to Vegas. I force myself to walk through the doors and the flash backs don't stop. The lobbies are almost identical, though this one is brighter, it's white but still has a large light fixture hanging dead centre. The floor is a gold and the seats velvet. The all-familiar lump in my throat reappears and I begin to question why I even thought it would be a good idea to step foot in another hotel until I see Doreen's face. I almost forgot how petite she was. Her little body sitting on the green velvet sofa opposite to me. Her face beaming, she stands and waves me over. I feel myself become very self conscious as I walk over, I instantly wrap my arms around my body.

'Sweetheart, you look well!' Doreen opens her arms out to me engulfing me into a hug.

'Thank you, so do you!' We both sit down, and she runs her hands through my hair. 'This colour suits you!' I can feel myself getting a little embarrassed.

'Thank you, Doreen. How was your flight?' She looks at me with such delight etched on her face. She gasps and places her hand on her chest.

'Oh, Darlin' it was amazing! That lovely brother of yours had me fly business class; I've never felt so lucky in all my life!' I look back at her with joy trying not to let on that I had no idea Charlie had paid for her flight here.

'I'm so happy that you're here.' I look at Doreen with pleading eyes. She looks back at me sympathetically.

'Shall we head into the restaurant?' Doreen breaks the emotional cloud hanging over our heads with one swift sentence.

The restaurant at the hotel in comparison to the hotel interior was bland. Based on the first impression I am unsure as to why Doreen is so keen to dine here. We take our seats, get our order taken by a very plucky young waiter and within thirty minutes of talking our food arrives. Interior, shocking. Food service, fast.

'How are you feeling about the trial?' Doreen takes a mouthful of spaghetti and asks me the dreaded question. I finish my mouthful of rice noodles and nod, very unconvincingly.

'I'm feeling okay about it. I mean, I haven't really thought about it. Other things have been cropping up that seem to be taking my attention away from it. I have written something though in case they ask me to stand. Which I'm sure they will. 'I start rambling and pushing the food around on my plate and I know that Doreen knows that I'm just rambling away, but she doesn't stop me or try to make me reel it in. She just lets me be.

'Is there anything you want me to say Katheryn? Or don't want me to say? I know this is a lot for you and it being only two days away I want to make sure we're on the same page. I don't want you going away honey. None of this was your fault.' I look up at her as she holds my hands across the table, her eyes glossy in the dimly lit restaurant.

'You can say anything and everything. I'm at peace with what's happened. You know, bar a few nightmares.' I try to make a joke, but it just makes Doreen look even more sorry for me. 'Wait, did you say two days? I thought it was in two weeks?' She frowns at me and tilts her head slightly as if she doesn't understand what I'm saying.

'No, it's always been booked for the 12th. Unless I've got the dates wrong?' Doreen frantically picks up her bag and rifles through looking for her diary whipping it out and flicking through the pages. 'It's definitely on the 12th.' She looks back at me, that pity not leaving her face.

'Why did he tell me two weeks?' I lean back in my chair and end up just staring at the messed-up meal in front of me. I see Doreen move forward ever so slightly in my peripheral vision. 'I'm sorry, you don't need to ask, I should've guessed when you came into town so early.' There's not much for Doreen to do to try to ease the situation so instead we just finish our meals, and she asks me about Sebastian.

'How's your boyfriend? Sebastian, is it?'

'He's good. He's been super supportive but recently he's constantly popping off somewhere. Either with Charlie or alone. I don't want to keep asking but it worries me slightly. I know all of this has been a lot for him too, but I can't help but think maybe he's- ' 'Don't even say that out loud.' Doreen cuts me off completely. I just take a deep breath and smile at her.

'How long are you staying for?'

''Til the end of the week. I can stay longer, for you.' It was meant to be a question but it comes across more of a statement without any choice needed from me.

'Thank you. I'll pay for your stay, of course.' Doreen shakes her head, almost ferociously.

'Absolutely no need. Your brother has sorted it all out. I will be forever in debt to you and Charlie.' Her words bring a lump to my throat and not I'm sure if it's there because her words were so touching or if I'm so mad that Charlie has gone behind my back and lied to me.

Multiple times.

'I'm glad we could help.' I say through gritted teeth. 'You do know you can come to me for anything?

I want to support you Doreen, for everything you've done for me, and my brother of course.' It even pains me to give him any kind of recognition especially after our 'altercation' earlier if you could even call it that.

'The thing is Katheryn; I didn't want to tell you like this but I'm not very well.' The waiter arrives at the most inappropriate time and clears our table. I can almost sense what's coming so I stand up and move my chair closer to hers. She puts her hands on top of mine. 'I've not been well for a very long time. It's cancer. Again.'

'Again?' I try searching her face for any kind of answer.

'I've had cancer twice, three times now and this time I'm not going to make it.' Her words are almost whispered at this point and unbeknown to me tears start individually falling down my face. Doreen gently wipes them away with her thumb.

'There's treatment Doreen. Let me pay for the best treatment we can find; you can beat this. You've done it before, why not now?' She simply shakes her head at me, a smile graces her face.

'It's too late sweetheart. I'm too old, there'd be no point.'

'Doreen! Please don't say that. There's always a point. It's your life.' My voice raises and a few heads turn our way.

'I've lived a good life Katheryn and helping you and Charlie have been a true blessing for me. I have no family, no children. I regard you two as my family.' As soon as the words leave her mouth, we are both crying. 'One thing I ask, don't tell Charlie yet. Just wait until the trial is over, once I'm home and in bed.' I lean away from my friend slightly.

'Only if you let me do one thing.' She raises her eyebrows at me. 'Let me find you somewhere to live in the city so I can look after you. So you have your family near you, for once.' She stifles a laugh and looks back at me like I'm a child and I've just proposed an idea of freezing her so she can live forever.

'Katheryn, I appreciate the sentiment, but I cannot afford to live in New York City!' I move forward once more.

'You won't have to worry about that. I will take care of everything. I'll be able to see you every day if you want, Charlie will be around too and Sebastian. You won't have to go through this alone. Not this time.' Doreen just stares at me with a blank face. She wipes under her eyes and straightens the trinket-y necklace hanging around her neck.

'I have no idea what I've done to deserve someone like you in my life.' A smile creeps onto my face and I end up beaming at Doreen.

'So that's a 'Yes' then?' She leans in to whisper into my ear.

'One condition. Don't make me live on the Upper East Side, I've heard pretty bad things about that place.' We both erupt into laughter.

'Come here.' I stand, ushering her to do the same and engulf her into a hug, her tiny frame allowing my arms to wrap right around her, her Chanel perfume filling my senses. 'Did you want to come back to my apartment? You can stay for dinner, and we'll drop you back here whenever you want to go.' Doreen affectionately rubs my arms and nods her head.

Chasing Echoes

'That would be lovely.'

12

Doreen fitted in perfectly to our little family. Within twenty minutes of being back at my apartment she had her shoes off and feet up on the coffee table, flirting with Sebastian watching some kind of rom com on the TV. Watching from the kitchen, it was like I was viewing the most wholesome scene. If I could live this every day for the rest of my life, I would. I take over a tray of teas and place them down on the side of the coffee table free from feet. We all take a mug each and I make myself comfortable in the armchair.

'Have you told Charlie I'm here or is it a surprise?'

Sebastian and I stare at each other briefly before I respond.

'He doesn't know you're here; it'll be a complete surprise!' Doreen isn't stupid, I should never forget that. She stares me out until I break the eye contact looking back at the tv. She lets me off the hook, just this one time, but I just know as soon as it comes back up again, I'm going to have to come clean.

After an hour and a half, the film eventually ends, and Charlie still isn't home. Sebastian and I keep sharing concerned looks and I know that Doreen keeps catching them too.

'You two gonna tell me what's going on?' She catches us both off guard and we both adjust in our seats.

'It's nothing really, Charlie had a go at me this morning and stormed out of the apartment and we haven't seen him since.' Doreen fully takes the mother role. She sits up and clasps her hands in her lap.

'I don't want to know details of whatever was said but have you at least tried contacting him?'

'I've tried his phone all afternoon while Kate was out, it just goes to voicemail.' Sebastian gets his phone out of his pocket. 'I've even sent text messages, but nothing.' Doreen sighs.

'He's an adult, I'm sure he'll be okay, though would it help if I gave him a call? I could meet him maybe and find out what's wrong?' I look at Doreen with a look in my eye that says 'absolutely not, not in your condition' but she stares me out and Sebastian gets in there first.

'He definitely would trust you more than us at this point, wouldn't hurt to try, right Kate?' He looks over at me and I'm still unsure. My leg starts bobbing up and down.

'Alright, there's a cafe just two doors down from here, you could meet him there?' Doreen shakes her head.

'No. I don't think he should know I've been here first; he'll know I've spoken to you first and think it's an ulterior motive. I'll meet him back at my hotel, if you'll be kind enough to get me a taxi. I have no idea how they work here.'

'Are you sure Doreen?' Sebastian turns to look at me as if to ask me why I'm worrying so much. To him Doreen has at least another 20 years left in her. Doreen stands and we both stand too, as if she's the Queen. If she stands, we stand. She walks over to me, places her hands on the sides of my arms once more and gives them a little squeeze.

'I'll be fine sweetheart. I'll message you as soon as I get back to the hotel.' I can't help but feel like I'm going to burst into tears as she looks at me. She lets go and slips her shoes on. Sebastian helps her put her coat on and she slings her bag over her shoulder.

'I've ordered you an Uber, he knows where you want to go, and it's all been paid for you so you don't have to do anything but get into the car. I'll take you down, he's outside.' Sebastian holds his arm out for her to link hers onto. Doreen certainly likes Sebastian. She loves the attention of a young man for sure.

'An Uber? What sort of taxi firm is that?' She waves me off as they both leave the apartment. I slink back into the armchair fighting everything inside of me not to cry but it's no good. I have a good old sob. I hear the elevator from outside pinging its way to my front door and I wipe my face, exhaling exponentially. The front door opens, and Sebastian returns to the apartment.

'Well, she's a legend.' He walks in and sits back down on the sofa. 'Come here.' I soppily move myself from one seat to the other and embed myself into my boyfriend. He places a kiss on my head, his signature move.

'He lied to me.'

'About what?' Our exchange is calm.

'The trial, Harvey's trial. It's in two days, not two weeks.' Sebastian's body doesn't react.

'What?' His voice didn't have any emotion in it. I instantly pull away from him. 'You knew, didn't you?' I stare at him demanding an answer. 'Kate...'

'Did you know or not.' Sebastian looked sad and I instantly knew the truth.

'He told me when we went away. I didn't want to

keep it from you, I didn't see the point, but he told me I had to keep it quiet. I'm so sorry, I didn't know what to do.' I move away completely.

'You tell me Sebastian. That's what you do. Why the fuck does he not want to tell me.

He doesn't want me to go, does he? Something else is going on isn't there? Tell me.' 'That's all I know.'

'Tell me you haven't heard from him today. Tell me you're at least not lying about that.' He looks at me with that same manner.

'Are you fucking kidding me!' I catapult from my seat and place myself to the other side of the living room.

'He's been with Maggie all day.' Sebastian barely gets the words out. He's cowering like a dog.

'Speak up!' My tone frightens him.

'He's with Maggie. He's been there all day.' I don't

stop pacing back and forth. 'And you don't think you needed to tell me? I don't want to sound selfish but all of this should involve me. This trial on Thursday is about Harvey and it's about me. I don't appreciate being cut out of everything that's going on. Don't you think I should know what's going on?' I stop pacing and pause. Deciding to choose my words carefully for this next blow. 'It's getting really hard to figure out where your dedication lies. Knowing that the two people I live with are keeping secrets from me that are about me and my future is not okay. I know you know what the phone call was about this morning, I know Charlie would have told you. I'm not going to ask, but this is not on Sebastian. I need to trust you. I understand you want to protect me and look after me, but this is too far now. I can't live with someone who doesn't tell me the truth. I can't live with someone that hurts me.' My voice cracks ever so slightly.

Sebastian stands and grabs me, fumbling over my hands. 'Kate, what are you saying?' 'I think maybe you should stay with your parents for a while. 'I regain my composure and stand strong with my words. He stutters and brings his hands up to my face. I back away. 'Kate, please. We were only trying to help you.'

'Help me? By keeping me in the dark with everything? You know, I don't care much about being kept in the dark about Louisa but about the fucking trial I'm meant to be attending? In TWO DAYS, SEBASTIAN! How were you going to tell me? Wake me up and say 'SURPRISE!'?' He shakes his head and goes back to fumbling over my hands. I step away from him once more leaving his hands empty. He bows his head.

'I'm sorry Kate. I am. Please, I love you.' He tries

to plead with me and as much as it breaks my heart, he can't stay here. Not in my house. Not for a while.

'I'm sorry too.' I still stand strong and the tension in the air is pierced by a notification going off from my phone. I pull it out of my jacket pocket and see Doreen is at the hotel safe and sound. Charlie has agreed to meet her. I look up to tell Sebastian, but he's already turned away, walking into the bedroom. I sit back down onto the sofa and send a quick reply to Doreen acknowledging her message and to ask how things went.

About ten minutes of aimlessly looking out of the window, I hear a small noise behind me. Sebastian drops two holdall bags down on to the floor and stands awkwardly by the front door. I reluctantly walk over to him and lean just as awkwardly on the arm of the sofa folding my arms in slight defence.

'I'll, um, text you when I get home then?' I nod.

'Yeah ok.' Sebastian leans in for a kiss, but I move my head away. He clears his throat and picks his bags up. I open the front door and he gets in the lift. He turns around and gives me a half-hearted smile. I return the gesture and close the door.

It's not until I walk into my bedroom where I notice the true absence. I thought I would be sadder, but the anger is still bubbling away under my skin. Despite the emptier wardrobe and the lack of shoes left by his side of the bed I don't fully feel like anything has happened. I take my denim jacket off and lay on the bed. I end up taking an impromptu nap until I'm woken up by the feeling of someone sitting on the end of my bed.

Charlie leans over and places a cup of green tea on my bedside table. I sit up and fix my hair behind my ears. We both awkwardly sit in silence waiting for the other to speak.

Guess that's what you get from two kids with traumatised childhoods.

'I'm sorry for earlier. I didn't mean anything of what I said. 'I take a sip of the tea. 'It's fine.'

'Stop saying it's fine when I can see you're angry. I'm sorry for lying to you about the trial. I know you know. I shouldn't have lied to you about that, I don't really know what I was thinking. It's just with everything and how you've been feeling, I thought it might take the pressure off if I didn't tell you it was sooner rather than later and then all of this with Louisa.' It seems rambling runs in our blood but he's right I'm still dead angry.

'One thing though.' I place my cup of tea back down on the bedside table. 'Why did you make

Sebastian lie to me?' Charlie runs his hand over his face.

'To protect you I suppose.' I shake my head and I see him looking around noticing the room a little emptier than before. I cut in just before he asks the question.

'I told him to leave. He's gone to stay with his parents.' 'Kate.' Charlie says my name as if to make me feel guilty.

'I can't trust someone who's willing to lie to me and then sleep in the same bed as me.' 'And what about me then? Are you going to kick me out too, I've done a hell of a lot more lying than he has.'

'No. Not yet. Firstly, you're going to tell me everything I don't know. No skimping on the details, no missing anything out because you'll think it might upset me. Just tell me straight up.' He looks at me in slight shock but eases his expression slowly. 'Alright. You better come to the dining room then.'

13

I've been sitting at the dining table for ten minutes when Charlie walks out of his bedroom with a black document box. You know the ones that when you unclip them, they burst open like an accordion. He sits opposite me and springs the box open. He starts pulling out different documents. Photocopies of photocopies. He then jolts up.

'Wait there, I forgot something.' I watch him sprint to his room and back again, holding a leather-bound book. A diary of some sort. He places it down on the table as he sits, opening it using the ribbon holding the chosen page down.

'Ready?' He nods at me, and I lean back into the chair making myself comfortable for the onslaught of information that's about to be thrown at me. Charlie pushes forward two pieces of photocopied paper. I look at them without moving my body forward, almost too scared to look at them.

'These are the affidavits that were found. Both within a month of each other. You can see Louisa changed her statement.' He pushes them further towards me and I finally lean forward and read them. The second statement is somewhat more heartbreaking to read than the first truthful one. 'Notice the dates?' I nod and make a mental note. Charlie then pushes another photocopied piece of paper over the table splitting the two statements apart. 'This is a copy of his accounts from September that year. The same month the new affidavit was submitted.' I grab the information in front of me and inspect it hoping I wouldn't see what we have feared. But there it was. A transfer of fifty thousand dollars to Miss L Jones. Fifty thousand dollars to keep her silence. Fifty thousand dollars to make her keep a baby she didn't even consent to.

The apartment is silent once again and Charlie lets me take in the information. I look up and open my mouth to speak a few times, but nothing seems to come out. I place the document down and push it away leaning back into my chair once more.

'A part of me didn't think he would you know? I used to feel sorry for him growing up. Eleanor used to treat him like shit. He could never get a word in, but I guess now I know why.'

'Don't you start sympathising with Eleanor. She's not innocent in this.'

'Is anyone in this family? I think you might be the

only one.' We both chuckle at the stark reality of my comment and he pulls another three documents out of the box.

'These are Eleanor's accounts, sixteen years-worth. The first one being the year that I was born.' I take all three documents and place them in front of me. Luckily, I don't have to search through much thanks to the fact that the information I need has been highlighted bright yellow.

1985 - A deposit of fifty thousand dollars 1986 - 1997 A deposit of one hundred thousand dollars each year. 1997 - 2020 - A deposit of two hundred thousand dollars each year. All from William Simmonds Snr.

'She's been bleeding him dry!' Charlie raises his eyebrows in agreement.

'The weirdest thing is, she's not even doing

anything with the money. It's just in a random bank account. She has just over five million dollars sitting around doing nothing.'

'You're kidding?' He shakes his head and clears his throat.

'So, I spent all of the day today with Maggie. I've started proceedings to get her to agree to temporarily sign her assets to me.' He sees the confusion etched on my face. 'It basically means I will oversee everything she owns, including that money. Technically I'm not obliged to give anything back to her when she leaves prison, but by the looks of things, I doubt she'll be leaving prison at all.' I look at him in shock.

'You've really got this under control, haven't you?' 'I'm sorry I didn't include you.' 'No more apologising.' He laughs at me. 'Doreen is really our guardian angel, isn't she?' 'Oh, you saw her?'

'Katheryn. Playing dumb doesn't suit you. I know you set that up.'

'Was it nice to see her?' Charlie folds his arms and leans back in his chair.

'It was, she seems frail somehow. She was trying to act like herself, but I could just tell something was up. Did she say anything to you?' We both stare each other out until I start clearing the documents away to one side.

'She told me not to tell you until she went out of town or at least until the trial was over.' Before I even had a chance to take a breath Charlie had jumped in.

'The cancer is back, isn't it?' I just look at him with sad eyes. 'How bad?'

'It's terminal. Charlie I'm sorry.' Knowing how much of a mother figure Doreen was and is to my brother, it breaks my heart to know he's losing another.

He begins to talk but his voice just breaks as he does. 'I've already offered for her to move to the city so we can look after her. I said I'd pay for everything, and she's agreed.' Temporary relief washes over his face until the sadness returns.

'She shouldn't be alone. Why not have her move in here?'

'There's only two rooms Charlie.' Without missing a beat, he has an answer.

'I'll sleep on the sofa. I don't care. She can't go through this alone, at least she'll have twenty-four hour care if she needs it. I'll call her now and tell her I'm on the way.'

'Charlie, wait! Are you sure about this? We have a lot going on and I'm not saying I don't want to help her but is this the right environment for her?'

'It's better than being alone surely? After all she's

done for us. It's the least we could do.' I take a deep breath and nod my head and mime a silent 'alright' and Charlie is automatically on the phone.

I pack all the documents on the dining table away back into Charlie's accordion -esque box and close it neatly, leaving it to one side. Charlie has walked into the sitting room and all I can hear is him persuading Doreen to come and live with us and to my surprise it doesn't take much convincing. Once I get a thumbs up from my brother I head straight into his bedroom and change the sheets as he leaves to pick her up. I move his clothes and other boy things into my room, filling the space Sebastian left. I take a few unused candles and a half a bouquet of flowers I have in my room and put them in a vase in Doreen's new room. I add extra blankets just in case and after twenty minutes of making sure everything looks homely for her the front door opens. I walk out into the hallway and see Charlie holding the door open as she walks in, her feet shuffling a little worse than earlier in the day.

'Welcome home!'

—⚬—

There's nothing like the feeling of looking after someone who once did the same for you.

Seeing the joy in their face when you take them on an open top bus tour through the city, pointing out all the places she wants to visit before she 'kicks the bucket' (her words not mine). Doreen's first full day in NYC with us truly exhausted her which in hindsight we should've thought about more as I'm now sitting on the edge of her bed with a cup of tea on the morning of the trial that she's agreed to speak at.

'Doreen? If you're not well enough to go today, it's

alright. Don't force yourself.' The sleeves of her night gown roll up as she pushes herself up in bed and I finally see how thin her arms are.

'Sweetheart, I'm fine, just give me half hour and I'll be up and raring to go.' She holds out her hands to grab the tea and I willingly give it over.

'When you say you're terminally ill, how terminal?' I try to be discreet with my wording, but it ends up not making any sense at all. Thankfully she understands.

'Not long now Katheryn. A month if I'm lucky.' My eyes start to well up, but I hold it together.

'How long have you known you were ill?'

'About a week after you left the motel. It's just getting worse and worse. I can feel my body giving up. It's an odd feeling Katheryn, I wouldn't wish this on anybody.' I move to sit next to Doreen and put my arms around her.

'You'll be alright now Doreen. You have us.' We have a moment of just embracing each other as if we'll never get the chance again, savouring every moment. She eventually pulls away and slaps me playfully on the leg.

'Go get ready you. You've got a big day.' I look at her and smile.

'Yes ma'am.' I leave closing her door gently and walking back into my room just as Charlie opens the door already in his black suit.

'Bedroom is all yours, how is she?' He whispers the last part.

'Not good. She said she's only got a month left at best.' Charlie just grabs me and hugs me tight, exhaling before letting me go.

'Go get ready and I'll make some breakfast.' We part ways and I shut the bedroom door, swallowing down any sign of emotion. I walk to the wardrobe and pull out a navy-blue jumpsuit and pair it with some matching ballet pumps. I straighten my hair, pushing it behind my ears and paint my face with minimal makeup but enough to show I'm wearing something. I smooth the clothes down onto my body once more in front of the mirror before taking a deep breath and heading out towards the kitchen. Though before I even get halfway down the corridor Charlie is rushing towards me with his phone clutched in his hands. Without being given any time to even ask what was wrong, he ushers me into my bedroom, firmly closing the door.

'What's going on?' I sit down on the end of the bed watching him check his phone multiple times. He's jittery and not in a good way.

'The trial. It's off.' His words are blunt and don't help me in anyway.

'What? Why? What's Harvey done now?' My questions seem to stop him in his tracks. 'He's killed himself.'

14

It's almost as if the air gets sucked out of the room the second those words drop. I feel instantly nauseous. Now don't get me wrong, he's an asshole. Or was. He shouldn't have sexually assaulted me. He shouldn't have killed Joe. But does that mean he deserves to feel so bad that he thinks the best thing to do is to kill himself? Did he deserve that? I can't decide.

Charlie's phone rings as I digest the information lingering in the air.

'Hi. Yes, I've told her. Of course. One second.'

He sits down next to me and puts his phone on loudspeaker. 'Okay Maggie, go ahead.'

'Thanks, Charlie. Katheryn, how're you doing?' I stutter. How am I meant to reply? 'I'm fine. I think. What's happening?'

'Harvey's body was found this morning at his apartment. It's been confirmed he killed himself.'

'Can I ask how?' Charlie snaps his head to me. God knows why I need to know.

'He hung himself.' Why did I even ask? My stomach begins to churn. 'He left a note. That's why I wanted to talk to you both. He left a note confessing to Joe's murder and to sexually assaulting you, Katheryn. I thought it might bring you some kind of peace knowing that he did eventually confess. Though now he's died, the case will get dismissed. I'm sorry to share such news with you both. Please let me know if there's anything I can do.' I stay silent as my whole body tenses up. Charlie notices and takes the lead.

'Thank you, Maggie. I'll be in touch in a couple of days.' Charlie ends the call and I dart out of the room and straight into the bathroom attempting to close the door at the same time. I end up crouched around the bowl of the toilet throwing up uncontrollably. There's a small knock on the door but I silence it, with my retching not hearing the footsteps entering the bathroom. I feel someone pull my hair away from my face and luckily, I relax slightly. I lean my back against the bathtub and to my side Charlie is doing just the same. He brings his arm around me and cradles me into his side. I burst into tears instantly, a mix of sadness and shock, relief and exhaustion. My brother just holds me on the bathroom floor not needing an explanation. It was only when we heard shuffling feet coming towards us that we both zoned back into reality. We both look up wiping our faces noticing Charlie had been crying with me when we see Doreen peering through the doorway all dressed in her best court attire including a pearl like necklace, adding a little glamour to the outfit.

'You alright, kids?' Charlie helps me stand up and we both escort Doreen to the sofa with her clasping on to each of our arms.

'You've got a day off Dor. The trial is off.' Us three all sit down on the sofa, side by side. Her head almost snaps over to me with such sorrow in her eyes.

'Oh no Katheryn, they haven't?!' The pain in her voice is unbearable. I clasp her hands into mine and shake my head.

'No, no, I'm not going anywhere. I'm fine, I'm staying here. It's Harvey. He's...died.'

It is hard for the words to leave my mouth as if I don't believe it still. Doreen looks to Charlie and he just nods his head to confirm the truth.

'It's a shame, but I'm glad you're alright sweetheart. Not to be grateful he's dead but I'm glad I can go back to bed.' We chuckle as we all sort of relax a little now the news has settled. 'Charlie darlin' would you mind walking me back to my room, I'm not feeling too clever on my feet today.' Without saying a word, Charlie stands and helps Doreen up, letting her snake her arm around his and they both slowly walk back to her room.

I slip my shoes off and walk into the kitchen, grabbing a bottle of water out of the fridge, gulping the whole thing down as quick as I was able. Turns out I'm more dehydrated than I thought. Death really takes it out of you. Charlie appears in the kitchen with a concerned look on his face.

'She's really not good today. Maybe we over did it yesterday?' I nod in agreement. 'I think so too. We'll let her rest today but if she doesn't get better, we might have to call a nurse.' Charlie sighs and mutters a small 'yeah'.

'Have you told Sebastian? Wasn't he going to come today?' I shrug in response.

'I haven't spoken to him since he left. I'll drop him a text telling him it's off.' Charlie notices my body language change instantly as soon as Sebastian's name is mentioned.

'You ok?' He looks at me from under his brow. Classic Simmonds trait.

'I'm good.' I nod to try to solidify my words, but it seems to just prove I am not 'good'.

Charlie takes a seat at the kitchen island; his body language is completely open. I sigh, knowing exactly what he's doing and knowing exactly how I fall into his trap every time.

'Like, what happens now? I know since all of this started, I've been saying how I just want to go back to normal, but now I have it, well if you ignore Eleanor and William's impending trial, I don't know how to handle it. Do we just go about our lives as if nothing happened? I know Harvey was a bad man and did bad things but all I can think about is how I caused another man to lose his life. I don't think I can live with that. I know I can't.'

'His death isn't your fault, Katheryn. Don't blame yourself for something you had nothing to do with. He couldn't even turn up in front of a court to plead guilty! He was a coward until the very end.' That last sentence triggered something in me. Anger.

'Killing yourself doesn't make you a coward Charlie.' I look at him questioning if I even know him at all.

'I didn't mean that. I just meant Harvey was never one to pay the consequences of his actions. Don't get me wrong, it's sad that he felt he should kill himself, but he never did help himself, did he?' I stand just absorbing what Charlie said, feeling completely conflicted. I step forward and lean slightly on the island opposite my brother.

'Do you remember when I dyed my hair? I completely submerged myself under the water and Sebastian thought I had drowned myself and pulled me out of the bath? If I had drowned before the trial, would you have called me a coward?' My tone is cold and hushed. I stare at him, and I can see the cogs turning in his head. I push away from the counter and walk down the corridor towards my room. I make it halfway down the hallway before he finally speaks.

'But that's different Katheryn. You were washing your hair. You didn't do that to kill yourself.' I stop in my tracks and turn around.

'Didn't I?' Before Charlie could retaliate, I turn my back to him and lock myself into my bedroom. It takes Charlie approximately seven minutes and forty-three seconds to knock on my door. Enough time for me to clean the makeup off my face and get into my favourite blue soft oversized jumper and grey joggers. I let him wait thirty seconds before opening my door to him.

'You can't drop shit like that and expect me to leave it.' Charlie whispers to not wake Doreen. He almost pushes me out of the way and makes himself comfy on my bed. He's also spent the last seven minutes and forty-three seconds getting dressed into his comfy clothes, surprisingly also grey joggers but instead a grey t-shirt. He pats the empty side of the bed next to him for me to join. I jump up and make myself comfortable for an extremely uncomfortable conversation.

'What do you want me to say?' I try to avoid his eye contact by pulling a cushion from behind me and wrapping my arms around it.

'Did you mean what you said or were you just trying to get a reaction out of me?' We both talk quietly for the sake of Doreen in the next room, which is nice to know as he won't be able to get mad enough to raise his voice. Is it normal for people to get mad when you tell them you have suicidal ideation? I have no idea, it's all I've ever known.

'It's partly true.' My focus is fully on the white cotton cushion in my lap, which is not interesting at all. Charlie tries to control the sigh that's leaving his lips.

'If you want me to be open and honest and communicate with you, you're going to need to do the same Katy. I'm your brother, I want to know if you're feeling low. I need to know.' I swallow hard and take a deep breath.

'Partly true in the fact that, in that moment I wasn't planning on doing it then. I never used to have baths, I used to hate them but when the panic attacks started, I found myself indulging in them. When things got bad with Mum, Eleanor sorry, I would run a bath and submerge myself and see how long I could hold my breath. There was something comforting about it. I didn't do it all the time, but just when things got tough. So naturally when things got tough this past year, I would run a bath but the thought of never coming back up for air? Yeah. It definitely crossed my mind more than once.'

'Do you feel like that now?'

'It's hard to explain. I want to say it comes and goes but in reality, it's just there. Some days are louder than others. I'm ok though.' I finally look up at my brother.

'Stop trying to convince yourself that you're okay. It's ok to not be. The past year aside, growing up hasn't been easy for you and I can tell you find it difficult to understand that yourself because of the environment you grew up in. Wealthy, big houses to sleep in, food whenever you want it, but it doesn't mean you're not susceptible to suffering with your mental health.' Annoyingly, he's right. Mental illness doesn't discriminate, and I do feel like I shouldn't feel like I do. The fact I've been using a coping method of holding my breath under water just to cope isn't normal and as I'm talking about it out loud it truly dawns on me how I'm not coping. I nod my head, not knowing what to say in response. Charlie holds my hand and looks back at me. 'If things get too much, if you get overwhelmed, if you find yourself getting into a bath and not wanting to come out, you can tell me. I won't give you a lecture, I know that doesn't help, but I will be here for you. No matter what.'

Charlie and I both hug but everything after that is all just a blur. Those words were all I ever needed to hear. Sebastian could've said those same words a hundred times over, but it wouldn't have felt the same. I could always feel the sentiment from Sebastian, but I guess it means more when it comes from family

15

It was 3am on Tuesday when I was woken up by the most bone chilling noise. I hop out of bed as quick as I can to investigate to see Charlie doing the same thing, just walking towards me from the sitting room. The whole apartment is silent, and we frown at each other before we hear it again. Our frowning faces turn to faces of terror as we both dart into Doreen's room and the sight that greeted us was not a happy one. Without even knowing it, Charlie and I both whispered 'Fuck' and rushed to her side.

'Doreen, can you hear me?' Her body was cradled into the fetal position and the white pillow lying under her head was now spotted with blood coming from her nose and mouth.

Charlie pushed her hair out of her face, and she was quite clearly in pain, her eyes shut tight in agony. She grabs Charlie's hand and I step away, my back against the chest of drawers just watching everything unfold in front of me.

Doreen mimes something to Charlie. Her words nothing but strained breath. She screams out in pain as she grabs tighter onto Charlie, coughing up more blood. He turns around to look at me, tears in his eyes.

'Call an ambulance.' Without a single word I leap to my room grabbing my phone, not even noticing how badly I was shaking and phone 911. Walking back into Doreen's room, I explain everything to the paramedic on the phone. He confirms they'll be someone with us within twenty minutes. I place the phone down on the side and kneel next to Charlie, in front of Doreen.

'Paramedics are coming Doreen. Just hold on. We're right here with you.' Tears start falling from her eyes as her body slowly starts relaxing from being so tense. Charlie continues to affectionately push the hair out of her face, which just shows more dried blood on her face. A knock at the front door allows me to avoid the situation and I jog to the door.

'Thank you for coming so quickly. She's in the room down the corridor, first on your left.' Two paramedics hastily make their way into Doreen's room, and I follow on hesitantly behind, leaning myself in the doorway, watching everything happen as if it wasn't really happening. I wasn't really listening, and I wasn't really watching what was happening, I was just staring at Doreen lying there. The only sign of life was her wheezing. She wasn't lying when she said she didn't have long left. Foolish of me to think she was overreacting.

'Kate?' Charlie breaks me out of my trance as he places his hands on my shoulders, bending down slightly to match my height. I simply blink a few times and I regain my own consciousness to focus on Charlie, and by the look on his face he's probably said my name a few times before I responded. 'They're going to take Doreen into hospital. I'm going to go with her, will you be ok here?' One of the paramedics pushes past us to get a stretcher from the ambulance. We both move out into the corridor.

'Yeah, I'll be fine. Make sure they look after her and keep me updated.' Charlie's eyes are still filled with tears. He might just be the strongest person I know. How has he not cried yet? He grabs me and pulls me into him, holding me tight in a cuddle, burying his head into my shoulder and that's when I feel his chest expand quickly and slowly my pajama top gets a little wetter. He pulls away trying to compose myself.

'Sorry.' He shakes his head, running his hand over his face. I pull his hands off of his face and wipe his tears with my hand.

'Never apologise. She'll be ok. She's in safe hands and she has you by her side. There's nowhere better.'

'Sorry to interrupt, but we're ready to go.' The paramedic ushers Charlie to follow him before my brother turns back around to me.

'Get some rest and I'll call you as soon as I get any news.' I nod and see them all out of the door and as soon as the front door closes, I notice the deafening silence echoing around the apartment. Everything happened so quickly that it's almost like nothing happened at all.

There's no way I can get any rest until I hear back from Charlie. I stand with my back against the front door and within ten minutes of me standing there I feel myself going into auto pilot mode. I shake away any sadness lingering in my body and go back into Doreen's room.

I strip the bed of the bloodied bed linen and replace it with fresh linen. I make the bed and lay the blankets and cushions on top as if it's going to be greeting Doreen this evening, when deep down I fear she won't be leaving the hospital at all. Despite it being gone 4am, I open the curtains. Nothing but the streetlights glaring through giving the room a cosy orange glow. Doreen's perfume still radiates throughout the house as I bundle the dirty sheets into the wash bin with no energy to get them to the washing machine. Instead, I take myself back to my bed and wrap myself up into my duvet, making sure I leave my phone's ringtone on loud and place it on the bedside table. I fight the tiredness until I eventually sink down into my bed just hoping everything is going to be alright.

The morning sun streams into the apartment and blinds me as I open my eyes. I subconsciously grab my phone off of the bedside table. Not a single notification. 9am and not a single message from Charlie. I instantly call him, but it just rings off. I leave it a few minutes before trying again and finally I get through. His voice is tired and sad.

'Kate, I'm so sorry I didn't text, my phone died, and I've only just charged it. I've just spoken with the doctor.' Charlie panics his way through the conversation.

'It's alright, is everything ok? I've just woken up, is there any news?' I sit up in bed as Charlie clears his throat.

'Um, the cancer. It's moved to her lungs. They've advised for us to stay here today. They don't think it's going to be long.' My heart sinks at the news, my throat closes slightly just at the thought of losing Doreen. I try to sound stable on the phone but with no luck.

'Okay. I'll make my way over; shall I bring anything?' 'No, just yourself. She needs her family now.'

The thing about cancer is that when someone is diagnosed, you're given time. Time to process, time to understand, time to live, time to slow down, time to speed up and do everything you've wanted, but no matter how much time you're given or not given, you still never expect that person die. You never expect them to leave your world. I hate everyone that says, 'well it was expected'. Well, no not really, because despite being terminally diagnosed, there is always hope. You hear about these amazing humans who have been terminally diagnosed that beat the odds and live much longer, much healthier lives, living with the disease and you think, 'well why can't my mother do that?' 'Why can't my father do that?' 'Why not my sister?' 'Why not my brother?' 'Why not my child?' 'Why not the woman that saved my life?' As brutal as it is, I feel it is simply down to luck of the draw. You can be the strongest person in the world but still die from cancer. But even then, there is still hope.

You just have to hope that that person lived a good life, did all they wanted in their life, whether long or short. Make sure that they didn't die with regrets. Make sure they died knowing they were loved, but most of all make sure you get to say goodbye and have hope that one day you'll get to see them again.

16

Four hours is all it took. Four hours of Charlie and I sitting at her bedside, watching her chest rise and fall until it didn't anymore. Everything was silent and still as we get a cab back to the apartment. I watch the cars go past, the people walking on the sidewalk as my brother and I are sat here in some kind of time halting emotional black hole. Why are the people walking past not noticing our sadness? Do they know that Doreen died? Do they not care about the fact that the one person that looked after us and miraculously bought us together has left this earth?

Grief is a funny thing. Makes you think you're the

only one in the world going through it. Makes you think you're the only person who's lost anyone. Makes you angry and sad and happy all at once. Which is a bit of a tough thing to handle when you have two people who don't communicate their emotions in one household who are both grieving. Yes, I'm calling myself out - that's progress.

'Do you think we should start thinking about arranging a funeral?' I say as I chop some strawberries into a bowl. I hesitantly ask, knowing how delicate the subject is and seeing as neither of us have mentioned it in the three days since her passing. I thought over breakfast might be a good way of starting. Charlie sits on the other side of the kitchen island staring at his phone. He puts it down on the counter as soon as he hears my question. He sighs. 'I suppose so.' His response was void of any feeling. A bit like his whole body has been since tragedy hit. I don't rise to his nonchalant reply.

'We can have a small one at the local church? Do you know if she wanted to be buried or cremated?' Charlie lets out a small huff, almost laughing.

'Kate, she had no family. It's just going to be me and you. I have no idea what she wanted; we just have to guess.' I just nod and carry on preparing breakfast. Dolloping some yoghurt into a bowl and throwing a handful of fruit on top, I slide the bowl over to Charlie, hoping he catches it, also hoping he doesn't, and it goes all over him. Sadly, he catches it just in time.

'You good?' Charlie looks at me in slight shock as he cradles the bowl in front of him. 'Mhmm. I just don't appreciate being spoken to like that. We're both sad. We're both upset. We've both lost someone dear to us. Don't make me feel shit for wanting to give Doreen a good send off. Family or not.' Charlie's face softens. He pushes the bowl back to safety, leaning forward.

'I'm sorry Kate. We could have a small ceremony at the church up the road. I can call them later and see if we can book something?' I walk around the kitchen island and sit on the stool next to him with my breakfast.

'Thank you. I'm not asking you to arrange it, we can do it together, but please don't treat me like crap, we're both in the same boat.'

'I know, I'm sorry.' He pills me into his side. I pull away and notice the bags under his eyes, darker than ever.

'How long are you going to sleep on that sofa?' He instantly averts his eye contact and becomes fidgety.

'Until we move. I can't even walk into the spare room let alone sleep in there.' My heart breaks at the honesty. I haven't even been able to step into the room since we came back without her. I just nod my head and take another spoonful of yoghurt. I can't argue with that.

Charlie's phone starts vibrating on the table, taking us both by surprise. He drops his spoon into his bowl and picks up the phone, showing me the screen before he answers.

Maggie.

'Hi, Maggie.' Charlie answers with doubt lingering in his voice. With an accumulation of 'Yeses', 'Right oks' and 'Ohs', Charlie quickly ends the call and holds the phone in his hand before he looks at me. My face mirroring his.

'Well?'

'Eleanor and William's court hearing. The final one, it's tomorrow.' 'Can they do that?

Can they schedule it so soon?'

'Apparently, they sent us a letter informing us. Maggie was calling me to see if we were going to go because we hadn't told her.' We both look behind us and see the pile of unopened post from the last three days sitting on the coffee table. We both turn and look at each other.

'We should really open our post. Do we have to do anything?'

'No. Just attend.' My eyes widen in surprise. Surprise is probably the wrong word. Shock? Relief? Disbelief? 'Plus, they have our statements, we just have to sit there, that's if you want to go. You don't have to.'

'No, I want to. I'm ready to see this through.'

We both finish our breakfast and I make it my mission of the day to open all of the post waiting for us while Charlie calls the local funeral arrangers. Majority of the post was junk mail, the one letter about the trial tomorrow and one suspicious looking A4 brown envelope addressed to both Charlie and me.

Sitting on the floor, I reluctantly open it. There's something about seeing a large brown envelope amongst small white ones that makes one feel a little apprehensive. I tear it open and pull out an official looking letter. Official, purely down to the fact its card-like paper with an embossed letterhead.

'Charlie?' I practically shout his name through the apartment. He comes running into the sitting room, toothbrush in mouth. Clearly, I caught him mid-brushing.

'What?' Speaking with his mouth full, he wipes toothpaste from his face.

'This was in the pile. A letter from Doreen's solicitors. They're requesting us to go down to the office for a will reading?' Charlie bobs down next to me and reads it.

'It's in Vegas, on Friday.'

'In three days, Friday?' He just nods at me.

'We can't not go. There's something she must want us to know.' I lean back into the bottom of the sofa, sighing as I go.

'When it rains it really does pour.'

'I'll book the flights, we'll come back same day, yeah?' I silently agree by just smiling back at him and he scurries back to the bathroom to finish getting ready for the day. I gather the post, leaving the important mail on the coffee table and taking the others to the bin before heading to my room to get ready for the day.

Once dressed, I walk back to the living room to find Charlie watching TV on the sofa. I grab the laptop from the kitchen counter and sit down next to Charlie. It takes Charlie about ten minutes to start looking over my shoulder and another fifteen before he starts asking questions.

'Houses?'

'Yep.' He nudges me with his elbow.

'You're not leaving me, are you?' His comment was half joking and half serious. Damn, we're a real double act with some serious abandonment issues.

'Of course not, you idiot. Looking for that fresh start, remember? Wanna go back to Cali? Or go somewhere brand new?'

'California. You'll like living there. Shouldn't we wait a little before moving?' I frown at him.

'What do you mean? I can buy somewhere in California for us and then sell this place, I have enough money.'

'I know you do, but maybe wait for after the trial at least. Just wait to know where we stand with them. Wait until we get the green light on starting a new life.' I sink down into the sofa, deflated.

'Okay. I just don't like the idea of you sleeping out here until the moment comes that we are allowed to move. At least have my bed for the next couple of nights, and I'll sleep out here?'

'Nope. You keep your room, it's only a couple of nights and then we're going to Vegas. It's fine Katy.' I could tell from the bags under his eyes and the occasional grunt from him when he stands up that sleeping on the sofa was not fine.

The morning of the hearing, I'm calmer than I thought. A weird sense of Deja Vu lingers throughout the apartment as Charlie and I both wear the exact same outfits as we did just last week. Thankfully, the trial is the first one of the day so luckily, we don't get much time to overthink, though there is enough time for a Starbucks on the drive to the courthouse. After a short journey we pull into the car park and wait. The atmosphere in the car is a comfortable silence but the kind of silence that screams at you to say something. I try not to give in but exhale louder than anticipated. Charlie looks over at me as he unclips his seatbelt.

'Anxious?' I shake my head. I think for the first time I'm not anxious. Why is the feeling of not being anxious giving me anxiety?

'No, I'm alright. Are you?' He nods and sinks his back into the chair.

'Honestly? I'm happy they're going to trial, but I can safely say from the bottom of my heart that I couldn't care less about what happens to them from this day forward.' He stutters. 'Sorry I know you're not there yet.'

'No, I get it. You've had twenty years. It's not even been a year yet. Don't get me wrong, I could never forgive them, just give me time.' Charlie nods and looks at his watch.

'Shall we?'

17

The courtroom itself was intimidating even without people filling it's seats. The walls were half dark wooden paneling while the top half was bright white paint. Seventy's style lights hang from the ceiling, making everything almost fluorescent, and if you look into them, you'd sure as hell be blinded. Five minutes before court is called and the courtroom is barely full.

Charlie and I sit on the second row from the front and Maggie joins us. A few people walk in and take their seats in the rows on the other side of the room.

After a few moments of waiting with intense

anticipation, a side door near the Judge's chair opens and out hobbles one man, handcuffed, and a woman strutting as best she can in an orange jumpsuit and sneakers, both being escorted by a burley police officer each. William clocks Charlie instantly and then looks over at me. His left eye black, clearly a fresh punch to the face. He tries to smile at us, but I look down into my lap, clutching my hands together.

Charlie does the same but places his hand over mine, squeezing it slightly. Eleanor and William both sit down at the same table, their lawyer sitting in between them, which by the looks of it is not one they hired. We all rise as the judge walks in, Charlie's hand not leaving mine.

I'm sure important words are spoken to the room but I'm not paying attention at all.

The sterile atmosphere seems to completely

disorientate me, and all that's keeping me within this room is feeling Charlie occasionally squeeze my hand.

Eleanor and William's lawyer, dressed in a very basic grey pant suit with a black strappy top underneath, stands, clearing her throat and holding a small dossier of papers.

'After recent discussions with my clients, it is in their best interest to plead guilty to all charges.' She walks up to the judge's seat and hands the dossier over his desk before sitting back down between the two culprits.

Charlie, Maggie, and I all look at each other in complete shock. After weeks and weeks of pleading not guilty they've given in, and dare I say it, taken responsibility? Now there's a turn of events. Maggie shakes her head at Charlie and I as a sign to remove the looks of shock from our faces in case there's press cottoning on to who we are.

'Based on the evidence given over the last few weeks and in light to the most recent evidence gathered, I have come to a decision. Eleanor Simmonds please stand.' My heart leaps into my mouth. 'Eleanor Simmonds, it is without any doubt that everything you have done over the last thirty-six years has been premeditated and all for monetary gain. Not once did you have any concern for the welfare of the children in your care, nor did you care once for the biological mother of those children who you watched her drown to death. In light of this, I am charging you with manslaughter as well as offences including fraud and deceit. You will be sentenced to twenty years in prison. You will be sent to the closest female facility where you will complete your time with no chances of appeal.' Eleanor just stands there and takes it. I look at her body language from behind and not one word from the judge wounds her. Two police officers appear behind them.

'William Simmonds, please stand.' William stands with help from leaning on the table for support. His posture is hunched. 'In fear of repeating myself, you are not an innocent man.

I am, today, charging you with two counts of rape, offences including fraud and deceit, obstruction of justice, and manslaughter. You will be sentenced to thirty years and will spend your sentence at the facility at which you are currently being held. You are not granted an appeal.' Nothing seems to phase William either, though a small amount of feeling shows in his body language, as his head drops when his sentence is announced.

Before I can even fathom the outcome of the hearing, two police officers are escorting William and Eleanor out of the courtroom and we're all standing as the judge leaves the room. The room empties quicker than expected and it's like a scene from a movie but also not. It's like an odd parallel and not as exciting at all. Maggie and Charlie go to leave but my legs have other ideas and I sit myself back down. Still holding Charlie's hand, he pulls me, thinking I am walking behind him, but I simply let go. Charlie is too busy talking to Maggie to notice until he turns around and sees me staring into thin air.

'Kate?' I can hear him but I'm not registering it fully. My whole face is frowning and I'm blinking as if to make sense of what I've just heard. 'Kate?' His voice is softer as he moves to sit next to me once more.

'Thirty years. He'll be dead.' Charlie places his hand on my leg reassuringly.

'You don't need to worry about that Katy. They both got what they deserved. Come on.' He stands again and ushers me out back to the car. Maggie says her goodbye in the parking lot and we both get in the car. I rest my head against the car window as Charlie drives us home in silence. We'd been on the road for thirty minutes longer than usual when I realise we're driving through the centre of New York City, nowhere near Brooklyn. I sit up in the passenger seat and look over to Charlie who's absentmindedly driving through the city (and when I say driving, I mean constantly stopping and starting his way through the traffic).

'Where are we going?'

'I was wondering when you were going to notice!' He says in jest. I laugh back at his comment.

'You're taking literally the longest and hardest way home!'

'I just thought we could grab some lunch.' I look at him suspiciously, the tone of his suggestion has me feeling apprehensive. We luckily find a place to park on the street, Charlie pays the meter and literally drags me down the road, my arm linked with his. We reach the lunch spot he chose and from the outside it looks just like a regular cafe. I step inside and I can't help my laugh and simultaneously punch him in the arm.

The inside of the cafe was decorated in full 50's style. So much better than the one in Nevada, this one actually had customers and the staff were dressed in full 50's costume. We were sat down once more in a red booth, this one had leather that was almost brand new and there was a bright multi coloured jukebox in the corner, free for anyone to use. There was even a disco ball hanging above it. Each table had a red Cadillac car acting as a napkin dispenser. I stop looking around and see Charlie looking back at me with a smirk on his face.

'I thought it would be nice, you know like old times?' I hold back a laugh. 'Old times like when your name was Frank and I carried a gun around with me?' 'That's the one!' We both laugh out loud and the thought that if anyone else could hear us laughing over this, they'd for sure lock us up. I rest my head in my hands, elbows on the table, thinking about the day.

'So, this is it huh?' Charlie mimics me. 'Whatcha mean?'

'Do you not find it odd? Like after everything, everything, that Harvey's dead, Eleanor and William have been sentenced, the whole, your mother isn't your mother, the fact that we're sitting here, relatively unscathed, it almost doesn't feel right? No one in this world would ever understand any of this if I were to open up to them. It's just me and you now.' I whisper the last part as if I'm harbouring a massive secret, which I guess I am. Charlie relaxes into his seat a little.

'I know what you're trying to say Katy. This past year has been tough for you. You've been hanging onto a hurricane for so long and now it's stopped and it's uncomfortable because you've been so used to the chaos for so long that now it's not here you don't know what to do right?' Nail on the head.

'Yeah, like, where do we go from here?'

'Nevada?' I sigh, he's not getting the urgency in my tone. He notices and leans forward. 'Stop forcing yourself to have everything figured out. Stop trying to map the future out, take one day at a time. Focus on us going to Nevada for now and then we'll tackle the next thing, together.' I involuntarily relax into the booth as if I'm almost giving in but knowing that he's right. My brother is always right, at least when it comes to this stuff.

Before I can acknowledge what he's said, a waitress dressed in a baby pink 50's dress comes over and takes our order. Charlie orders the burger special, which is apparently New York City's largest burger, and I order turkey dinosaurs with curly fries with the chocolate milkshake special which Charlie makes a disapproving face towards. The milkshake arrives and the pile of cream is half of the fountain glass.

'Please don't throw up on the way home!' We both laugh.

'I'm not a kid, Charlie!' He raises his eyebrows and points at this monstrous milkshake in front of me.

'Says the girl who's just ordered a kids meal and the largest chocolate milkshake I've ever seen!'

'Okay, you have a fair point but I'm never going to say no to the opportunity of curly fries AND turkey dinosaurs!' And as if right on cue, our food arrives. Charlie's burger towering high and hilariously my kid's meal arriving on a small plate decorated with multi-coloured stars. Charlie covers his face with his hands in horror that his little sister is really doing this. 'Best day ever!'

The turkey dinosaurs and curly fries went down a treat and by the time I'd finished my meal Charlie wasn't even half-way through his. I finally make it through the mountain of cream and manage to sip some of the actual milkshake.

'You struggling?' I poke fun at Charlie having to take deep breaths between each bite of burger.

'I'm good.' I raise one of my eyebrows at him.

'I don't think it's me that's going to be throwing up in the car!' He leans back and runs his hand over his shirt, breathing out some more.

'Alright, my eyes are way too big for my belly, at least just this time.' I shake my head as he gives in, but he still takes an onion ring off his plate to eat, just to be sure.

'I'm just popping to the toilet, I'll be back in a second.' I grab my phone and walk over to the back of the diner and into the women's toilets or, as this establishment likes to call us, 'gals'.

There's a whole wall full of cubicles, each door and wall to the cubicles painted a baby pink. I can only assume the men's are painted a baby blue. I lock myself into one of the cubicles and put the seat down to sit on. I look at my phone screen and Sebastian's face is looking right at me.

The feeling of wanting to just give him a call and tell him everything is so strong. I drop him a message instead and hope that he doesn't hate me too much to text me back.

Hey, it's me. Are you free to talk? Thankfully, within twenty seconds he replies. Of course. Want me to call?

Actually, would it be okay if I called you at 7pm tonight? Sure. Hope you're okay. X I ignore the bluntness of the last message and don't bother responding as the thought that I've been in the toilet for longer than what's healthy crosses my mind. Charlie must be becoming suspicious. I unlock the door and walk back out into the diner. Charlie now sitting in the booth at an empty table, watches me walk back to the booth.

'You weren't throwing up, were you?' I make myself

comfortable back in the booth. 'No!' I try to avoid his eye contact, but I think he already knows what's going on. He doesn't question me any further and we pay the bill.

'How do you feel about setting off for Vegas in the morning?' Charlie's question takes me by surprise. I stutter my words a little.

'Er yeah, why not!' Without missing a beat, Charlie bounces forward with excitement. 'Thank god, because I've booked the flights and I've booked an Airbnb. The flight is at eight thirty, we'll get into Vegas at about half one and the meeting is booked for three, so we have some time to rest before.'

'Sounds perfect. What time are we leaving the apartment?' 'Aim for six?'

'Perfect.' Charlie smiles at me though his eyes are

questioning me. 'What's going on?' 'Nothing?' Charlie scoffs.

'Have you spoken to Sebastian?' I roll my eyes. I hate that I cannot lie.

'I just texted him. Asked if I could call him later. That's all.' Charlie just nods at me. 'Just to tell him about Doreen. Check he's okay.' His face pulls into a smile.

'As long as you're okay.'

'I am. Just focusing on Nevada.' I wink at him. But I am okay. Or at least I will be.

18

As soon as we got home, I slipped the formal clothes off and replaced them with my pajamas. I resigned myself to my bed the second I had the opportunity, which helped with the fact that I didn't have to succumb to watching the clock for seven o'clock to come round. The downside to my plan was that I was jolted awake by my phone ringing. Ten past seven and Sebastian's name is flashing up on my phone. Shit. I answer the phone before I've even sat up in bed, my voice slightly groggy. Not how I planned to greet him. My plan was to sound like I was doing well for myself, that I was coping and happy. Not that I've just taken a six-hour nap on a weekday. I clear my throat but forget to say hi.

'Kate?' It was so nice to hear his voice again. 'Sorry! Hi.'

'I didn't know if you still wanted to call so I thought I'd call you.' The exchange is awkward.

'No, I'm glad you did. I was napping and completely forgot.' Okay the last bit was a lie. I didn't' forget, I was avoiding.

'How've you been?' Sebastian breaks the thick ice lacing this phone call.

'I've been good. I wanted to talk and just let you know that Doreen passed away a few days ago.' There's nothing but silence on the other end of the line. 'I'm so sorry Kate, are you ok? What happened?'

'I'm alright, we're both alright. She had cancer. She moved in with us and Charlie and I looked after her for her last week or so. We're actually flying to Vegas tomorrow.'

'How come?' I'm not sure he really cares but perhaps he's just being polite. 'Reading of the will. We've been requested to go; I'm assuming because she has no family.'

'I hope it goes ok.' Everything is so very formal. Almost like we're both too afraid to let our guard down.

'Thanks. How have you been?' I guess it's only fair that I ask. 'Good, yeah good. Just back at home.'

'How are your parents?' Making small talk has never been either of our forte.

'Also good. They're actually on holiday at the moment, they've gone to St Lucia. It's their wedding anniversary.' I smile as if he'd be able to see me.

'That's lovely, send them my love.'

'I will. Any news on Harvey's trial?' I frown into

thin air. I can't help but think he's been living under a rock the past week. How does he not know? Harvey's death made the news. Globally. A knock on my door distracts me. Charlie's head pops through and he mimes saying that dinner is nearly ready before he pops back out again. I clear my throat and focus back on the phone call.

'Sorry Seb, I've got to go. Let's have a proper catch up when I'm back in the city?' He also clears his throat in turn as the words stutter out of his mouth.

'Yeah, yes sure. Let's do that.' I immediately end the call. I can't do goodbyes that awkward. I push my phone under my pillow and roll out of bed. The weight of pure unease has me almost slumping my way into the living room. Charlie takes one look at me as I take the bowl of pasta bake waiting for me off the coffee table and drop down into the sofa.

'Oh god. What happened?' His tone is slightly sarcastic with a tinge of disappointment laced throughout. I stuff a mouthful of dinner into my mouth.

'Nothing of note. It was just very awkward.' I try my best not to let any food leave my mouth as I talk with it full to the brim with pasta. Charlie just stares at me as I finish my mouthful, knowing full well there's more to this than I'm letting on. 'He asked about the trial.'

'William and Eleanor's?' I simply shake my head. 'No. Harvey's.' Charlie frowns harder than I did.

'But that's common knowledge. Everyone was reporting on his death. How does he not know?' I shrug my shoulders.

'I don't know. Maybe he was trying to make conversation? It's just odd.'

'Are you going to speak to him again, or is this it?' I

start playing around with my food and Charlie nudges me as he notices I've been pushing one piece of pasta to one side of the bowl to the other.

'I said we should meet and have a catch up once I get back to the city.' I rush what I'm saying in case Charlie has some adverse reaction to it but instead he just sits and nods.

'Okay. I'm here if you need me.' I smirk at him. 'As a chaperone?'

'Maybe. I'm kidding. Slightly. You made him leave for a reason. If you want him back in your life, make sure you have a good enough reason for that too.'

'I love him, and I know deep down he would never do anything to hurt me, not really. I was just angry. Angry at both of you. It made me feel sick to my stomach that the person I loved was lying to me but the more I think about it, I'm just as bad. Everything I didn't tell him about the past year. About life at home in general. They'd be nights I'd sneak out of the house and go to Sebastian's. I'd just turn up with a little bag of clothes, enough for a couple of nights, with no explanation, and he'd just let me stay, not asking any questions. I shouldn't have treated him like that just because I wasn't in control of the situation. I'm sorry to you too.

You've bent over backwards for me the past year and I haven't exactly been nice about it.' Charlie shuffles closer to me on the sofa.

'You need to stop apologising to me. I don't care anymore. We've both been shitty to each other, but I don't think you can blame us under the circumstances. Also, not that you're asking for my opinion, but as your brother, I think Sebastian is a good guy. He was the one bending over backwards for you.' Charlie brings me in for an awkward side hug.

'Have you ever been in love Charlie?' He sighs heavily. 'Maybe that's a story for another day.'

19

Las Vegas never ever fails to amaze me. Albeit my second time here, but it still fascinates me. Surrounded by all of this hot landscape and condensed right in the middle is the famous Vegas strip. Where the rich get richer, and poor get poorer. Perhaps the epicentre of capitalism.

We drop our bags down on the laminate flooring of the Airbnb's kitchen floor as soon as we get in. Both of us letting out a much-needed sigh. I turn around and see Charlie checking his watch.

'We've not got long to get freshened up. We've got to leave in twenty minutes max.'

I haul my slightly over packed holdall into one of the rooms and close the door behind me. Slipping into nicer jeans (basically ones without holes in) and tying my hair into a ponytail, the gravity of why we're here hits me. I almost want to say it comes in waves but that's absolutely the wrong analogy. It's more like it's always here, it being grief. It's always around you and sometimes you breathe out a little too much or you for one second stop holding your breath in hopes of keeping it all together and you become vulnerable for a split second and the grief wraps a hold around you and you feel all of the world's sadness at once and in that same split second you remember that person you lost and the sadness that overcomes your whole body is ten times worse than the weight of the world's sadness you're already feeling.

I readjust the ruby red ring on my finger, smooth some wispy hairs to stay put on my head and take a deep breath before heading back into the living room with every hope I can keep it together during the reading.

Grabbing my coat off the back of the sofa, I hold it in my arms as I watch Charlie come out of his room. It seems he had a moment in his room too as he takes a deep breath as he smooths his crisp shirt down walking into the living room to meet me.

'Shall we?' I simply nod at him, seeing right through him. Weirdly, it's reassuring knowing we're both in the same boat.

The Uber journey to the attorney's office is completely silent. The Simmonds trait of uncontrollable leg bobbing seems to be the only thing getting us both through. The car stops sooner than we both had hoped, and once more deep breaths were taken as we exited the car. Charlie and I stand outside the building for a few moments before heading in. A silent moment of reassurance. At least that's what I'm taking it as.

The office is nothing exciting. Your classic attorney's office. Again, I'm assuming.

What is an attorney's office meant to look like? An older man, with half a head of hair, and a navy-blue pinstripe suit approaches us as we sit in the reception area.

'Mr. Simmonds, Miss Simmonds?' He double checks the papers he has in his hands.

We nod and both say 'Yes' simultaneously. 'I'm Gerard Schroeder, Ms. Doreen Nash's attorney. Would you like to come to my office?' We both stand and follow him through the short corridor into a deceptively small office with just about enough room for three people.

Gerard Schroeder's office walls were decorated with many diplomas and degrees and the odd baseball in a Perspex box on his desk. Charlie and I sit on the other side of the desk, the room is so tight we are elbow to elbow. If it wasn't for the massive mahogany desk taking up most of the space, we'd probably be able to feel a bit more comfortable.

'Firstly, I'd like to start off by saying I'm so very sorry for your loss. Ms. Doreen was such a lovely woman and to have known her for so long personally, I know how much of a loss that is.'

'Thank you. That means a lot.' Charlie takes the lead in thanking this complete stranger. Gerard simply nods and takes a manilla envelope off his table and uses a letter opener to slice it open.

'It's not legally necessary to do this, however Ms. Nash amended her will four months before she passed and asked for this to be read to yourselves on the occasion of her death. Are you happy for me to proceed?'

'Absolutely.' Gerard pulls a white piece of paper straight out of the envelope and adjusts his glasses to sit on the end of his nose.

'I, Doreen Nash. being of sound mind and body do hereby declare that this document is my last will and testament.'

'Sorry, can we skip the legal jargon and get to why you've asked for us to come today?

Sorry to be abrupt but we have no idea why we're here.' Gerard looks up at Charlie with a shocked look on his face. He turns his attention to me briefly before reverting back to Charlie.

'Of course.' Gerard raises his eyebrows as he flips the piece of paper over revealing a second page stapled to it. He skims through the words until he gets to the important part.

'My assets both liquid and otherwise, I leave in their entirety to Charlie Simmonds. My entire ownership of Sunset Valley Motel, I leave fifty percent to Charlie Simmonds and fifty percent to Katheryn Simmonds. Likewise, the house at seven eight seven Orange Grove Boulevard, Pasadena, I leave in it's entirety to Katheryn and Charlie Simmonds.'

The air in the office seems to get a little thicker as soon as Gerard stops talking. My eyes are, from what I can tell from the tension on my face, twice as wide. I look over at Charlie and he's sporting the same facial expression, pure shock. Gerard clears his throat, noticing the lack of conversation coming from us and decides to take the lead by pushing two more manilla envelopes across the desk.

'We've made a copy for both of you to take home and within these envelopes are letters written by Doreen for you both individually. They haven't been touched since she's written them.'

'Thank you.' Charlie and I both grab the envelopes from the desk and hold them in our laps. 'Is there anything else we need to know?' Gerard shakes his head.

'No, that's all.'

'Was there anything about her funeral mentioned?' I have to ask.

'I'm afraid not, Miss Simmonds. She did not request anything.' I nod my head in acknowledgement.

'Thank you so much for your help.' Charlie stands

and shakes Gerard's hand. I follow and do the same. We shuffle out of the room and out of the building and linger on the sidewalk whilst we wait for another Uber. I run my fingers along the edges of the envelope in my hand.

'I guess we get to move to California after all.' I gingerly look up at my brother in case my words didn't land like I hoped but thankfully he laughs and wraps his arm around me, looking up to the sky.

'Are you sure you want to move? I know Doreen has left us her home and business but are you sure you're really ready, Kate?' I move so I'm facing Charlie directly, placing my hands on his arms.

'I'm one thousand percent sure. If anything, today has proved to me that it's the right thing to do. We're literally being given a fresh start, a new business, a new life. Are you ready?'

'You know I've never wanted to leave the west coast. I only came back to New York for you. I've never been more ready.' Right on cue our Uber arrived. This journey was so much less anxious, less leg bobbing and so much less silence. The car was full of conversation about plans for the motel we now own and how our living arrangements will be, considering it's a one bedroom home.

'We can just extend it Charlie; it wouldn't be that hard surely?'

'Kate, the house is surrounded by hundred-year-old trees and other small homes, extending it wouldn't be an option.'

'Extend it upwards then.' 'What?'

'Put another floor in, I don't know the technical terms, but go up instead of.out?' Charlie looks out of the window.

'I guess that could work. We need to properly plan it.'

'Or I could just buy a place nearby and live there and you live in the home you know, that you already live in...?'

'Katheryn, you can't keep buying property and not make any profit out of it. I know we're well off but we're not that well off.'

'No, I mean, I'll sell my Brooklyn apartment. I don't need it. I'm not going to live there anymore and that was the plan anyway. Then use the money I sell it for, for a place near you and any left-over money we can put towards revamping the motel. It needs some work if we're going to make it into a successful business.' Charlie just looks at me. No expression. No indication on how he could possibly react to my proposition.

'That's actually a good idea.' I sigh loudly. 'Don't act so surprised. Jeez.' Charlie laughs.

'No, I didn't mean it like that., I just mean it could actually work, if you're happy to do that.' I sigh even more.

'Charlie. I suggested the idea, of course I'm happy to do that.'

We pull up to the Airbnb and make our way inside. I almost forget the letters left for us inside the manilla envelopes given to us by the attorney until Charlie mentions it as he wanders into his bedroom to read his. I follow his lead and close my bedroom door behind me. I sit down on my bed as I take the contents of the envelope out. Two pages of official documents as read to us earlier and a small envelope with my name handwritten on the front. I carefully peel open the small envelope and pull out a smaller handwritten letter.

Dearest Katheryn,

I want to start by saying I am so proud of you and so happy that you came into my life. You and your brother mean the world to me. I have no family, no children, and I truly believe that God sent you both to my door as my children, just as much as you both needed a mother. I know my death probably won't be one where I get the opportunity to say goodbye and I didn't want to leave everything on such official terms so here is my goodbye.

There is nothing I want more than for your brother and you to be happy so please have the house and the motel. I know you both will be able to run it to the best that it was always meant to be.

Katheryn, forgive me for sticking my nose in, but as much of a strong woman you are, please know you are loved, by me, by your brother, and by Sebastian. That man loves you.

Don't ever let him go. Hold on to that love for the rest of your life.

There's nothing better in life than knowing you are loved. Thank you for showing me love and care for the small amount of time you impacted my life.

With all my love,

Doreen.

p.s, Look after your brother. You and Charlie are more alike than you think.

A few teardrops land on the paper, causing some of the ink to run. I attempt to dry the paper with my sleeve but to no avail. I lean over and grab my phone out of my bag.

Subconsciously scrolling through my contacts and putting the phone up to my ear as soon as it starts dialing out. An almost unrecognisable raspy voice answers.

'Sebastian?' He clears his throat and starts again.

'Katheryn? Hi!' I copy his actions and clear my throat in hopes it doesn't sound like I've been crying.

'Are you free to talk?'

'Of course, are you okay?'

'Yeah, I'm in Vegas. For the will reading. I just wanted to call to say, well I want to say something, but I don't know if it's going to be reciprocated so now I'm just rambling like an idiot and hoping you'll jump in any second and save me from falling down this massive hole of verbal diarrhea.' The voice from the other end of the phone is completely silent until his familiar laugh echoes through.

'What's going on Katy? Talk to me.'

'I miss you. And I really fucking love you. And I'm

really fucking sorry for treating you so badly when all you've done is support me and be there for me and not complained much at all considering the shit I've got you involved in.' I hear rustling through the phone as if what I've said has made him sit up right wherever he is.

'I've missed you so much, Katy. Last time we spoke I didn't know what to say or if you were completely over me. I couldn't tell where we were going. I love you. It's always only ever been you. You have no idea the things I've been doing just because I've missed you.' His confession manages to break me down completely. Almost as if it's released a huge weight off me.

'Are you still in town?'

'Yeah, I'm at my parents still. When do you get back?'

'Tomorrow, about 3, I think. We need to talk. Doreen left Charlie and I the motel and house.'

'Does that mean you're moving?'

'Yes. But I don't want to go without you.' Silence lingers before Sebastian musters up a response.

'Pasadena or Vegas?'

'Living in Pasadena. I'm going to sell the Brooklyn apartment and find somewhere near Charlie's. Look why don't you come over tomorrow evening, we can have dinner and talk about everything.'

'Alright. Just text me when you get back and I'll make my way over.'

'You don't have to come with me if you don't want to Sebastian. I don't want to force you.'

'I'm not a long-distance relationship kind of person Katy, you know that. I'd move to the ends of the earth for you. There's nothing I wouldn't do for you.'

20

Landing back in New York City felt somewhat bittersweet. A mix of feeling like I'm back home and feeling completely betrayed by the city, when in fact it was never the city that betrayed me. Walking through the doors of my apartment that kept me safe for the past five years knowing that in a few months will be home to someone else makes me feel sad. Nothing more nothing less, just sad.

I suppose being Simmonds children, Charlie and I seem to adapt to sudden change quite well. We both unpack, get into comfy clothes, put some washing on and immediately start preparing for dinner. Almost like both of our default settings are to appear normal and in control. God knows where we learnt that from.

'Do you think I should wear something nice?' I look down at the oversized jumper hanging off my body and the food-stained black joggers that are tucked into my multi- coloured fluffy socks as I ask Charlie the annoyingly obvious question. He looks at me trying his best to think of something supportive and endearing to say, knowing I won't like anything but the answer 'No'.

'I guess you can't really blame this look on jet lag, can you? Why don't you just go put some jeans on, a cosy top. Keep the socks though, they're truly something to behold.' He points down at my feet.

'Ugh, I hate that you're right.' I skulk off to my room doing exactly what Charlie says, rummaging through my closet to find my best attractive yet cosy jumper. Is there such a thing? As I'm tucking my favourite pastel jumper into my blue jeans, a knock at the front door grabs my attention. I peep a look through my bedroom door as Charlie opens the front door, and boy am I glad that I changed.

Sebastian waltzes into our apartment looking better than ever. His signature navy blue buttoned-down shirt with dark blue jeans and perfectly shined black shoes pulled my attention immediately. His freshly shaven face and freshly cut hair screams out to me that he's actually put an effort in to see me. Ok, that's a bit egotistical but surely, it's just pure logic and above all polite that I make just the same amount of effort? Glad we all agree.

I pull out my trusty blue and black floral wrap dress and quickly swap my clothes over.

I squeeze myself into some thick black tights and

take my hair down from the high scruffy bun on top of my head. I smooth my hair down before applying some very discreet mascara. I take a deep breath while I slip my feet into my slippers (it adds to the 'I haven't made any effort at all' plan) and finally exit my bedroom and walk down the hallway, where I find the two men nursing beers in the kitchen.

'Hey!' They both turn their attention to me, Sebastian looking just a little more interested in me than my brother, thankfully. I walk between them, leaning to get myself a beer from the fridge before turning back around to see Sebastian's eye contact hasn't left me.

'That's a nice dress. Is it new?' Charlie breaks the tension and stares at me as if he's up to something. I frown until the penny drops.

'No, I've had it for years, thank you.' I stare back

at him with all daggers leaving my eyes telling him to back off.

'Are you staying for dinner, Charlie?' Sebastian thankfully changes the subject.

'I thought I'd leave you two to it, you've got a lot to catch up, I'm heading out for a bit.' I scoff at him, staring him up and down.

'Looking like that? Who's the unlucky lady?' He raises his eyebrows at me. 'Two can play that game.' Charlie laughs and finishes his beer.

'On that note, I'm going to change and head out. Nice to see you again bud.' He slaps Sebastian on the shoulder before leaving the kitchen.

I gesture to Sebastian to head into the sitting room and he follows. We sit next to each other on the sofa, both of us sitting in silence for longer than we planned for.

'You look well. How have you been?' I try to break the ice. This tension is giving me first date vibes. He smiles at my attempt of small talk.

'I've been good. I've missed you.' He places his hand on my thigh. I meet his hand with mine and squeeze it ever so slightly.

'I've missed you too.' I lean in, and the smell of his cologne sends me back to how I felt when I first met him. The memory goes from black and white to full colour as he cups my face with his hand and kisses me so softly but with so much passion. He doesn't push his luck and pulls away after one kiss leaving me wanting more. I slowly open my eyes and his are staring back at me. He pushes my hair behind my ear, his voice hushed.

'I meant what I said, what I've always said. It's always been you and it always will be.' I kiss him once more, lingering my head on his. 'How soon are you moving?' I pull away slightly.

'I think Charlie wants to move back as soon as possible. I'm going to put this place up for sale as soon as I can.' Sebastian nods, taking the information in. 'I know it's a big move and a big change, we'd be back and forth from Vegas with the motel renovations and everything, so I don't expect you to make a decision now.'

'No, I want to move with you. I'm ready to leave this city too.' His eyes are dead set on mine and instantly it makes me feel excited that I get to start this new life with him by my side.

'We can make a house our home, get a car that is ours together, maybe the home will have a garden, we can have barbecues and fourth of July parties.'

'White picket fences and rose bushes?' 'Exactly that.'

'Do you have plans for the motel?' I take a sip of beer before answering.

'Not really, Charlie and I haven't really spoken much about our plans other than it needs a good refurb, it's pretty run down.

'I'm sure whatever you do with it, Doreen would love it.' I look down and find myself subconsciously playing with the ruby ring on my finger once again. I simply just nod and smile at Sebastian, feeling that all-familiar feeling in my throat, knowing the second I say something nice back I'll absolutely start sobbing. I clear my throat and stand up.

'Let me check on dinner.' I walk into the kitchen and notice Charlie already there and plating everything up. 'I didn't see you come in here, sorry you should've said and I would've helped.'

'Don't be silly! How's it going?' He whispers to me, in hopes of getting all the gossip. 'It's going fine. He wants to move with us.' Charlie's head couldn't have snapped to my attention quick enough. 'What?'

'What? What's the problem Charlie?' 'It's just soon that's all.'

'Soon?'

'You two have only just made up and now you're moving in together, leaving the state his family is in. That's a big commitment.' I sigh, staring up at the ceiling. 'Hey, I'm not saying you shouldn't do it or that it's a bad idea, just be cautious Katy. You're my baby sister and I don't want to see you getting hurt again.' He pulls me in for a hug.

'No, I understand. We'll be ok, I promise.'

21

Packing up the last few things in my apartment is a bittersweet moment. What was once my safe haven is now an empty shell of a home. I take a moment and sit in the middle of the floor next to the last box filled to the brim with stuff. I look around and see the plain walls that once had my favourite art prints, the large clock that once graced the wall by the window, all packed away. My favourite sofa that I bought purely for the colour and not for comfort, already on it's way to Pasadena. I find the lump in my throat reappearing ever so slowly as I think about how much this place means to me and ultimately how much it saved me.

Megan Gant

Long before finding Charlie, before Harvey Fernsby became an everyday name, and long before my mother wasn't my mother, this apartment was that one place I could escape to that no one knew about. It's like when you're a kid and your parents buy you a playhouse and that becomes the centre of everything. You make it your own by bringing in your favourite teddies and stick a handmade KEEP OUT sign to grace the front door because only you are allowed in. When you have a tantrum, that's where you'd run too. When you had no friends to play with, that's where you'd go. When you wanted attention from your parents because it felt like they forgot you existed, that's where you'd hide. But one day you notice you grow a little too big for your playhouse. From the outside world, you become a caricature with your arms hanging out of the windows and your head poking through the roof and all

Chasing Echoes

of a sudden you realise you've grown up and out of the home that was your one and only security, and now it's time to root yourself elsewhere. Find somewhere else that's big enough and strong enough to support you and your dreams. But what do you do when you're only used to walls made of plastic and windows that fly open? What happens when the whole time you've been living, not one person has respected your KEEP OUT sign and that privacy is just something that other people have? You start from the ground up. You start from scratch.

You build those walls yourself, with your own hands. You use your own strength and enrich every brick with the same strength that got you through those hard times. That's what will protect you. You add windows in that provide you with the air and space you need but know you have the power to close the window and create that boundary on your terms. You furnish your home with the things that make you happy and, in the end, you will have your safe haven. Stronger than ever. As you will be knowing you've got your own back. And that's what I'm doing. I bought a house for Sebastian and me to live in just across the street from Charlie.

The foundations are strong and that's a good place to start.

'You set to go?' Charlie strides into the apartment picking up the last box next to me, making me jump out of my daydream state. I clear my thoughts as I stand up, smoothing my hoodie down.

'Yeah, let's go.' I sigh, reaching into the pocket of my hoodie and pulling out the door key. I follow Charlie out before taking one more look at the empty apartment and lock the door behind me for one last time. Charlie holds the elevator open for me. I stand next to him as the elevator doors close and we make our way down to the ground floor.

'If this box wasn't so heavy, I'd pull you in for a hug.' I laugh and rest my head on his arm. 'You alright kiddo?' I sigh heavily.

'Being an adult sucks. Moving sucks. Everything sucks.'

'Not everything sucks, Katy. You're starting a whole new life in a whole new home. Not everything is bad.' The elevator doors open, and we both walk out on to the street, Charlie struggling more so than me.

'I know, I'm just going to miss this place.' I turn around and look up to the building as Charlie loads the last box into the truck, telling the removal men we're all done. The truck begins to set off and Charlie wanders behind me, putting his arm around me.'

'Let's get out of here.'

—✺—

Pulling up in the Uber outside the new house, everything looks perfect. The white picket fence I'd always dreamed of and the rose bushes lining the path up to the porch, though as soon as you enter through the front door, you're greeted with boxes from floor to ceiling filled with unfiltered stuff. I completely underestimated how much less space I'd have moving from a loft apartment to a small home in Pasadena, without even thinking about the fact Sebastian would also have belongings. As soon as I open the front door and we see the wall of boxes, Charlie's eyes widen.

'Yeah. I'm going to leave you to it. After helping you back your apartment up and flying five hours, this is now on you. I'll be at home.' I laugh at his honesty.

'Thank you for your help, I'll check in later.' He walks back down the pathway and crosses the road to his home before shouting 'Good Luck!' across the street.

I make my way into my new home and tip toe through the maze of boxes in front of me in hopes that I'll soon find Sebastian at some point. I wander into the freshly decorated kitchen and there sitting on the kitchen island was a disheveled-looking man staring at his phone, wearing an oversized plaid shirt and grey joggers, completely distracting me from the fact he's sitting ON the new kitchen island.

'Hey you.' I walk up and stand in between his legs, greeting him with a peck on the lips. He pulls me in for longer than I expected.

'How was your flight?'

'Good. Got about eight more boxes arriving tomorrow evening.'

'Eight?! How much stuff do you have?' Thankfully he's playfully complaining. 'At this point, I genuinely don't know, I think it's just going to be decor things, everything else is already here.' He nods and lands a kiss on my forehead before jumping down from the island.

'The bedroom is all unpacked apart from one of your boxes. It wasn't labelled so I opened it, sorry. I think it's some of your things from Eleanor and William's place. I didn't know what you wanted to do with it.' I follow him to the bedroom, seeing said box on the bed.

'You built the bed!' Sebastian turns around with an innocently proud look on his face. 'I did!' I pat him on the back patronisingly, before walking over to the box on the bed. I peek into it and quickly retreat.

'I'll go through it in a bit. What're you doing now?'

'Unpacking the kitchen. Or at least trying. Why do you have so many mugs? You literally lived alone for three years?'

'I went through a phase of collecting them. Leave me alone.' Sebastian laughs and walks back out of the room.

'I bloody love you.' Sebastian's words echo through our home as I close the bedroom door behind me.

I sit on the edge of the bed and open the box once more. The leather files of Charlie and I, birth certificates, and photo albums fill the cardboard box. Even just looking at the items on the surface brings back that familiar anxious feeling. So, I, without triggering myself any further, calmly I close the box, pick it up and try to push it under the bed. As I do, I find something gets in the way of me pushing the box right the way under the bed. I move to the floor to look under the bed, moving my box out of the way, I find another box in the way. I lean further under the bed to pull it out of the way.

Bringing it closer to my body as I sit on the floor, I see that Sebastian has marked it with his own name and the box has been taped shut multiple times. A thousand things begin to run around my mind. I need to respect his privacy just as he did with mine, but a part of me can't help but wonder what he could be hiding from me. It wouldn't be the first time he's hidden anything from me. We're meant to be starting a new life together with no secrets, no hidden bodies in the closet. So, it's only fair I open the box, right?

I start slowly picking at the tape on the sides of the

box trying to get some kind of end to come up so I can just peel the tape off. After chipping my nail polish off, I managed to grab an end and pull off three layers of tape all the way off, letting the box unfold right in front of me. I open it right up and see that there is a bundle of rope. I pull it out and, as it unravels in my lap, I notice that as it goes along there are different types of knots knotted into it. It finally ends and I check the box to be sure it's empty and there sitting at the bottom is more rope, yet this is tied like a noose.

I hold the noose in my hands tracing my fingers over the shape as my brain attempts to process whatever the fuck has just happened. I hear a crash in the kitchen and my head jolts to the door, praying Sebastian doesn't come in. I stand and open the door, still with the noose in my hand. I walk straight to the kitchen as if I'm on auto pilot. I see Sebastian up on a step ladder screwing the clock to the wall, his back to me. I stand there in silence just watching Him, praying that there's a perfectly innocent explanation as to why he has a noose hidden under our new bed in our new home and that he would no way jeopardise our new life like this. Not after everything. Not him. I feel a lump in my throat forming and the tears in my eyes bubbling up. Now or never.

'What's this?' My voice is calm, but every bone in my body feels as if they're shaking. Still up on the ladder Sebastian replies with nothing but happiness in his voice which simply breaks my heart.

'What's what, honey?' He steps down and turns around to face me and instantly his face drops.

'This.' I hold the tangled rope out, my hands now visibly shaking. I stare at the noose in my hands and then slowly the penny drops, and we stare at each other, drowning in the silence. My eyebrows furrow with so much more remorse than his, hoping to hell I haven't figured out what he's done. 'He didn't kill himself, did he?' Sebastian simply shakes his head.

'He needed to pay for what he did. I killed him. I made it look like suicide. I did this for you.' He takes a step forward reaching his hands out, but I immediately step away. His revelation leaves me feeling numb. I can't help but look at him with such confusion. Every little thing from the past few months running through my mind at lightning speed. I'm debilitated by the shock.

'I was told there was a confession note.'

Sebastian replies instantly and without any hesitation.

'I went to visit him, the night you told me to move out. We had a friendly chat. I asked him to write out his confession. I told him to do it so I could trust he'd plead guilty on the day, and he did. You know, I think he was genuinely sorry.' Sebastian's calm attitude in admitting to this makes me feel physically sick but there's one thing I must know.

'How did you do it?' He looks down at the floor and takes a deep breath before looking back at me. I clench the rope that's in my hand in hopes it'll give me stability in this situation.

'He walked over to his desk to write the confession note, I followed and thankfully he didn't sit down to write. I had the rope behind my back, I strangled him with it. I simply hooked and tied it to the light fitting, made it look like he hung himself. I placed the chair carefully knocked over by the side of him. Took my things and went.' The tears of pure fear are busting out of my eyes. I look down at the noose in my hands.

'And this?'

'Just practice. Needed to get it right.' I drop it on the floor and push past Sebastian, running to the sink before vomiting. Sebastian comes over and pushes my hair out of face. I push him away with such force he falls into the island.

'Don't touch me!' I try to catch my breath.

'Katy, please!' I wipe my mouth and stand facing him, as if this is some kind of duel. 'You killed him. You killed him, and you're fine about it.'

'I killed him for you.' His eyes pleading with me to understand that he did this as a gift to me. He runs his hands through my hair, edging closer to me. His thumbs wiping the sparse tears coming from my eyes. My breathing slowly goes back to normal as I feel his skin on mine. I look up into his eyes.

'For me?' My words are quiet, and I begin to feel that there's no point in fighting this.

I find myself falling into his body and he begins to wrap his arms around me. We stay in this silence for long enough until we start swaying on the spot. A knock on the door breaks us from whatever this is. I pick up the noose that's laying on the floor and stuff it in a cupboard, hiding it from any visitors. Sebastian watches me and I briefly nod and smooth my clothes as we both walk towards the front door.

I open the front door with a beaming smile, Sebastian standing right next to me doing the same, to a woman who must be in her seventies trying to fool everyone she's in her fifties, holding a basket of mini muffins with a red ribbon gracing the basket.

'Welcome to the neighbourhood. I just wanted to drop by and say 'Hi' and give you these. I'm Janet, I live next door!' My god she's enthusiastic. I take the basket of muffins and beam my smile even more so at her.

'Thanks so much. I'm Katheryn and this is Sebastian. Lovely to meet you.' Janet pokes her head through the door further than we want her to and Sebastian closes the gap with his body. Janet retreats and eyes us both up and down.

'Well, you must have a lot of unpacking to do, I'll leave you to it.' And with a brisk wave goodbye, she trots back to her own home. I slam the door shut and the smile drops from my face instantly. I make no comment to Sebastian and head straight back to the kitchen, flippantly putting the basket of mini muffins on the side. I take the noose out of the cupboard and charge to the bedroom, grabbing Sebastian's hand as I go, pulling him along.

The box surrounded by the excess rope is still sitting where I left it. I kneel down and Sebastian follows my, lead sitting opposite me. I roll up the excess rope and place it the box before placing the noose on the top. I look at Sebastian before pushing the box to him.

'Put this under the bed.' He frowns at me. 'Just put it under the bed and we'll get rid of it when we can.'

'Are you sure?'

'Sebastian, just do it.' He pushes the box under the bed and takes my box of belongings and pushes that under too. He turns back to me.

'I'd be a bit of a hypocrite if I were to leave you now. We're in this together. Just no more murdering people.'

'In this together. Forever. Though, tell me you wanted to murder Janet? Just a little bit?'

'Oh god. I think adjusting from living in New York

to Pasadena is going to be tough. No one can be that friendly We'll make an exception for Janet.'

'Fuck Janet'

THE END

Ingram Content Group UK Ltd.
Milton Keynes UK
UKHW012004140323
418553UK00004B/457